The Unknown Kid

I0526695

Michael Pomeroy

Published by
Best Global Publishing
P.O. Box 9366
Brentwood
Essex
CM13 1ZT
United Kingdom

www.bestglobalpublishing.com

Dedication

For true friends from the Vine Christian School, C.P.B.C., CCIW and Elvian School. Also thanks to Martin Hopley who told me never to give up.

The Unknown Kid

Contents

Prologue

It is the year 2068 and the world is in chaos. The mafia's and groups of crime joined together and broke into the prisons all over the world. They had decided that they were ready to take over. Unfortunately for them, they were not very good at working together. They managed to break out the prisons, but they fell apart with disagreements before they could take down the major governments. After the world wide break-out, security was tightened and it was almost impossible to go anywhere with a governmental or political look to it. Politicians practically lived in the buildings they worked in because it was too dangerous for them to go outside. Crime was everywhere; gangs would roam the streets at night looking for innocent victims. The police could do nothing about it since they were stretched to their limit just trying to protect the politicians themselves, schools, and any buildings that were venerable or desperately needed protecting. The army were doing major jobs such as stopping major criminals and figureheads entering the country and illegal immigrants with ideas of helping out with the "bad guys". No one was safe.

The governments were in uproar. They were run dry for money since they were putting so much into protecting themselves. A large part of this money was going toward a new project that was their only hope. Nothing on earth could help them, so they looked for help from off the Earth. They used the latest technology to force down a meteor that was passing by to try and find new technology. The meteor came down in the Sahara Desert. They investigated the meteor and from it they found a new source of weird energy called elemancilin, a new substance that they used to make new prisons and weapons with.

But some of the technology went missing, as did a few guards and engineers, with some found dead in suspicious ways. A new figurehead has appeared in Reading, and no one knows who he or she is or what his target is. All they know is that he goes by the name of the 'Evil San.'

So Mick Denning, no. 1 spy in the S.P.F.T. for the Berkshire district is called in to try and find out what is happening.

This is one of many tales in the life of the Unknown Kid. There are many before this one, and many after. But this is the first that I will recount. I have studied the life of this one individual with much intensity, and I have researched his entire life. Through this research, I find that his teenage years are the best of stories for today's audience. The tales that I will retell for you are those that make this man who he is today: a legend and a hero. So here is the first chapter of the Obsolete story: his confrontation with the Evil San, and his gradual beginning of understanding the power of elemancilin.

Michael Pomeroy

The Evil San

The date is January 28th 2068

'Operation Hydra is going ahead on schedule, I presume?' Said a lazy voice from the high-backed chair. In the middle of the room stood a man. He was in his late twenties, and his face was rather large. His chin had a large amount of stubble on it from two days of not shaving.

'Oh, yes, sir, a few minor glitches but these should only affect the launch date by a week or so.'

'A week! Are you sure?'

'Almost positive sir.'

'Well it had better be shorter,' the voice replied. 'For your sake. If it is over that date, then I am afraid I'll have to fire you, literally, and replace you with someone more reliable.'

The chair turned around. A young man... or was it a boy? ... was sat in the chair. His face was horribly raw and disfigured from a burn that covered the whole right hand side of his face, his neck and, from what was not covered by his black shirt, upper torso.

'I have planned to get my revenge. It must not be delayed for too long. If so, MI5 will find out what I am doing. They are not so dumb as to pass it by. We have killed three of their agents. Now they are bound to send someone I won't expect. Or at least, they think I won't expect. There are two people who that could be. Unfortunately for them, I knew them for a while.'

'John Corton and Mick Denning,' the middle-aged man put in.

'Exactly, Doctor Feanam,' continued the boy. 'The most likely option is that they send both of them, with Mick as the leader and John as back up. Very unfortunately they do not know who I am. It is true that most of the time the tactic of sending kids would work; not many people would know about the S.P.F.T. section of MI5. If they were any other teenagers, it would take me some trouble to work out who it is was. But as I said, I was good friends with the two boys. Once. Get Tomodan to put all the assassins on stand-by by nine hundred hours tomorrow morning. By then Mick and John should be ready to 'test my security' and to try and bring me out to play. I'll play all right. We'll play 'go fish'. And I will catch them hook, line, and sinker!'

He stopped to think, and then, as if he had just come out of a daydream, realized that Mr. Feanam was still there.

'Oh, you can go Dr. Feanam. And make sure that that completion date is **on schedule.**' He put emphasis on the last two words.

'Yes Master Hunsan. I will get the men back to work immediately.'

He backed out of the room. When the door was closed behind him, he leaned on the wall and thought all about that he had heard in that room. Threatened death on himself, deaths of many secret agents, and two young boys meddling in the business of adults. It was all very disturbing. He now wondered what he had got himself into. That was another thing he needed to know: why was a teenager bossing everyone about and in charge of the operation?

Then he wondered what was going to happen to John Corton and Mick Denning. What horrible fate awaited Mick, or John? Or both of them? In fact, Mick Denning, at that very moment, was in a life-threatening situation of his own.

9/11 Again!?

At that very moment, 14 year old Mick Denning was in the doorway of a plane ready to jump out and save his life.

But to understand where we are in the life of Mick Denning, we will need to go back to the beginning.

Mick was a 14 year old teenager that did not follow the crowd. He had a different fashion, different hairstyle, different life style, different everything. He had a very different fashion sense. He kept it simple. Mick wore a simple t-shirt and jeans, with a jacket or hoody when it got colder. He did not like this new idea of wearing torn garments, sometimes not knowing if they were even actual clothes and not just piece of fabric to cover up the bare essentials. Others opted for the crazy style, similar to the 1970's.

Neither did Mick like the hair styles, which had crazy shapes and crazy colours. Mick had his flat and straight. It was blond mostly, and he had a long fringe. He gelled his hair when he felt like it and it could then take many forms. His body was in good physical shape too. People did not exercise as much, as nobody wanted to be out after sundown, which was particularly difficult in winter.

His lifestyle was understandably different, because he was a spy for the S.P.F.T.

Mick had joined MI5 and Scotland Yard a few years earlier. He was a whiz with computers. He had hacked into the files of Scotland Yard and he had seen how much chaos it was in. A new form of technology had somehow been found from a meteor that had landed on the outskirts of the

Sahara desert. It had given them a substance (called Elemancilin) nothing to what Earth had at that time. It had been discovered that Elemancilin could be solid, liquid, gas, or novenicity; a new form of energy, like electricity. Mick could not even come close to grasping how it worked. To him, it was like something out of a science-fiction movie. But it was just what everyone needed.

Mick had also seen the amount of people committing crime and how much strain was on Scotland Yard and MI5 trying to keep them at bay. He had not known how bad it was since the British government was using the media to cover it up. It was very difficult for them, since everyone saw the crime every day. But with discouraging the people from travelling and not telling them what was going on in the rest of the world, everyone thought it was only their area that was bad.

A new branch of spies had been set up called S.P. which stood for "Spy Police" . It was so called because the men who acted in it were spies, but had the powers of the police force. This branch was used to get rid of the heads of the criminal organizations because it was too much work for the police force, who were dealing with the constant crime, and the spy network had not the powers to do all that was needed. S.P.F.T. (which stood for Spy Police for Teenagers) was yet another branch off of the Spy Police. This teenager section had been made because it supplied more people and it was a way of getting in more easily than usual. It was also unsuspected, since not many people had heard about it, joined, *and* qualified the entrance tests.

So the new branch was made and from what Mick could see, it had been quite successful so far. It was all down to an anonymous pair who founded it as well as funded it, and Mick thanked them for doing so, whoever they were. Even though Mick had never had a big mission like a couple of agents had, he was still the number one teenage agent in the Berkshire region, and third ranking in England for S.P.F.T.

Mick had always had a fancy for the spying sort of thing. He had learnt martial arts, had been clay pigeon shooting and paintballing to practice his aim with a gun safely, and had always wanted to be the hero of the day. What Mick didn't realize was that in a few months, he would have to be a hero, or be zero.

* * *

Mick jumped out the door of the aeroplane.

Mick had been on that aeroplane because MI5 had contacted him about half an hour before to tell him that an attempt on hijacking a plane that had been expected for a little while had gone ahead. They were planning to do a 9/11; but in Britain! The hijackers planned to crash into Big Ben, making it fall onto the Houses of Parliament. MI5 had contacted him because the plane was about to fly over his house. Reading was a major fly-by route for aeroplanes going to and from London.

He ran to the local airfield about five minutes down the road, and got a plane and pilot to take him up. They flew up into the sky and saw a single plane. Odd. It was obviously that plane that he wanted since it was in the radius the air force had sent him it could be in, so he flew after it. He flew up alongside the plane, but the hijackers did not see him.

He got his pilot to hold the plane steady, and grabbed his gun. He grabbed one of the leather handles hanging from the ceiling and kicked the door open. A rush of air swept out of the plane, but Mick held onto his strap. He fired his gun at a spot near the other plane's door. Out shot a suction cup and wire. It hit the plane and stuck. Mick attached the wire to his plane, and then climbed along it to the other plane.

He eventually got to the door, got inside, and knocked out all of the guards (Now this is an important fact about Mick Denning. He made it a rule that he never killed on purpose, since he was a Christian. So MI5 had given him a modified P88 that took thin needles with a little anaesthetic in the middle that was injected into the person it hit, knocking them out. Each one shot could hold up to 5 of these needles, but Mick designed different needles, depending on the gun and situation, and loaded them with however many or few he wanted).

He gave control back to the pilots once he had revived them, but when he had made his way back into the main compartment, he found the guards stirring. Only then did he remember that he had only put 'half an hour' knock-out darts into his gun. Mick reached the door and jumped just as the guards realized what was happening.

* * *

As he fell, Mick's watch alarm went off. What was that for? Then he remembered. He had recently changed schools and that alarm was to remind him that he should leave to help with interviews. The interviews were to determine whether or not the children got in. All schools were like this because there were so many bullies and trouble-makers that they had to make sure that they did not let them in, because it was very possible that one or more of their parents were in one of the local gangs. If a certain student did not like a certain teacher, then that teacher's whole family was in danger.

Mick brought himself back to reality. He looked up and saw the hijackers peering out of the door. Then they jumped to. He looked at his altimeter, suddenly realizing he needed to deploy his parachute, and deployed it. As usual, there was the sudden jerk.

Once he had settled down, Mick looked around. He was now floating safely under the blossoming silk canopy. He looked around and tried to see where the plane had taken him. He found out that it had taken him over the M4. That was lucky. His school wasn't far off from junction 11 off the M4 and he was between that junction and junction 10. Mick steered himself towards J11. Soon enough, he saw it, on the opposite side of a business store. As he approached it he saw a car pull into the quite empty car park.

'*Must be another possible for the school*,' Mick thought.

Then he heard a cry behind him. As he looked round, he saw what he most feared; the terrorists were gaining on him! They had deployed their parachutes later than him, giving them the edge. His only hope was that he could get inside the building quick enough to gather himself together and deal with them in his own time, instead of them coming at him and he having no time to defend himself.

So Mick, being the genius that he was, figured out a plan. The distance to the building, the car, and the people getting out of it; it was all perfect.

He turned himself upside down.

'Wait for it, wait for it,' Mick muttered to himself.

He pulled on the release cord (it was a different type to the ones usually used at the time). It worked! The parachute came free. Now it was freefall from there to the ground. Suddenly he heard a bang and a bullet whizzed past his shoulder. So, it was now or never.

The timing could not have been better. The door was closing; it was now no less than a metre wide! Mick dived through. As he was about to land, he hit his hand against the latch. It had worked!

There was one problem though. When Mick was diving for the door, he forgot that he was at an angle. This meant that his momentum would take him forward... a lot. His pace had been extremely fast and it wasn't going to be easy to stop. Mick landed on his hands and flipped over. Now he was skidding towards the newly arrived people. He wasn't going to stop in time! His shoes hardly had any friction! Summoning all the energy he had left he flipped over the family and landed facing them (he had reached a wall to stop himself).

'Err, hi,' he said to the newcomers, looking through his fringe which he eventually put aside.

'Um, hi, nice to meet you,' said the mother, a little taken aback. There was herself, and who was obviously her husband and three kids; two girls and a boy.

'How do you do?' Asked the husband, offering Mick his hand. 'I'm Daniel; Daniel Baker. This is my wife, Lucy, and my kids, Katrina, Ana, and

Harry. We have a young one but he is asleep in the car. By the way; who are you?'

'Sorry to be rude,' Mick replied taking the hand. 'I am Mick Denning, a pupil of the school. Would you like to go into the waiting room? If you go through this door to my left and then the second door on the right.'

'Thank you very much', said the older girl. She looked about 14 years old. The other two looked about 11 and 9, with the latter being the boy.

'I would hurry if I were you, before...' He was cut off mid-sentence as a torrent of bullets hit the door. Luckily for the Bakers, they had already moved towards the door Mick had indicated, and were therefore out of the line of fire. But what about Mick? What had happened to him?

Mick got up off the floor, brushing the debris off his back. There in the wall behind him was a nice row of bullet holes. The middle part of the door was now torn to shreds.

'GO!' He yelled at them. They didn't need to be told twice. They ran straight through the door as Mick turned to the torn apart door. He got his gun out and reloaded it with more long lasting ammunition in it. When he felt ready, he opened the door and faced the terrorists. He got outside and one of terrorists started talking with a think European accent.

'You ruined everything,' said the man (who must have been the leader of the group), 'and now we will ruin you!'

Out came his gun. But Mick was quicker. Mick always carried two Beretta 92FS's with him. His guns flashed and banged once. Thin little needle darts were then protruding out of the leader, machine gunner, and a normal terrorist.

The terrorists had wasted most of their guns, so now they came on for unarmed combat.

'*Bring 'em on!*' He thought, and fired again.

Another two stumbled and fell. The other needle went nowhere. Mick holstered his guns and got into his karate stance. Since the terrorists wanted to fight karate style, so would he.

Obviously, the men had not been expecting to get into combat, not even a shoot-up. They were all ready to sacrifice themselves to take out the government, but then Mick had showed up and taught them a thing or two. At the start there had been ten men. Now, only half of them were left.

The first two to reach Mick went down with hefty blows to the temple, and the third got a roundhouse kick in the stomach, winding him and a punch to the head took him out.

One was hiding; the other was facing Mick and was obviously ready for the challenge. They circled each other, waiting for one to make the first move.

* * *

Whilst all this had been happening, the Baker family had run into the waiting room to find a single child with her parents and a family of 3 kids with their mother. Katrina Baker had always been inquisitive; poking her nose into things that probably weren't her business. When she had seen Mick, he had seemed odd to her. Where had he come from? She hadn't heard him come in. And why, almost as soon as he arrived, had bullets ripped the door apart and then he going outside towards the people shooting? It just didn't make sense, and she wanted it to.

19

'Mum, I'm just going to the toilet; I'll be back in a minute.' Katrina said to her mother.

'Sure sweetheart, but do not be too long. You've got your interview in a minute.' Her mother replied.

'O.K.'

Katrina headed as if to go to the toilet, but at the last moment she turned round and headed towards the front door. She arrived and peeped through the large hole that had now appeared in the door. The things she saw stunned her. The first thing that drew her attention was the amount of bodies littered on the pavement. There must have been at least 6, probably more. The next thing she saw was the boy who had named himself as Mick circling what *looked* like the last man standing. The last thing she saw, and the most deadly to her, *was* the last man, out of sight to Mick, and looking at her; raising a gun.

* * *

In fact, Mick could see what was going on, and, in a second, he had his gun out. As he fired at the man he was already fighting, that man also fired a concealed gun. The bullet just shaved the top of Mick's head bringing a trickle of blood to his hair. But Mick had the better aim. His shot hit the man square in the chest, and he collapsed.

But at the moment, none of that mattered. He charged forward and grabbed one of the thick metal bin lids that were lying there. The last man now had his gun pointing at Katrina, her eyes full of fear. Mick threw the bin lid into the man's line of fire. The terrorist became distracted by the bin lid travelling threw his line of fire and it caused him to pull the trigger prematurely. The bullet hit the bin lid, went straight threw it, but was sent flying straight over Katrina's head. With his last round, Mick shot the last terrorist.

The 9/11 reconfigured plot had failed.

'You should not have come to see what I was doing.' Mick said.

'Sorry, I couldn't help it,' Katrina replied. 'But you're hurt! You will need someone to look at that. My mum knows first aid.'

'Nah, it's ok. Just forget about it. Come on, I'll show you round the school.' He badly wanted to change the subject.

At that moment, Mick's mobile rang.

'Excuse me.' He said.

He walked off a little way to answer it. He looked at the caller. It read 'boss'. He answered it.

'Yes boss, what is it?'

'Hello Mick. Can you come in for a little chat? At last, we have a big 'man' (means assignment) for you. I'm expecting you want it? I can give it to someone else if you do not?'

'Oh no, sir, I'll take it!' His voice was full of enthusiasm. It was his first ever big mission, and he had been waiting a while for one to turn up.

'And by the way, how did the last 'man' go? You've finished it, I'm sure?

'The last 'man' is dead.' Mick replied with a laugh. 'Too many questions! I'll be with you in about a half an hour. Oh, some waste for you to deal with here boss; just outside school.'

'We will come and pick it up for you. See you then,' the boss replied.

Mick hung up.

He turned back to Katrina who had been patiently waiting.

'I'm afraid that tour will have to wait. I have to go see the head from my old school.' Mick lied.

'But what about your interview?' Katrina queried.

'Weren't you listening? I said I was a pupil at the school. That must mean I have already had my interview and have been accepted,' Mick replied. 'Anyway, hope to see you in the school.'

'Yeah, see you later!'

Mick turned and walked away to see his boss and to find out what this big assignment was.

John Corton

Mick was a few streets away from his house after walking from school, he saw a familiar figure walking towards him.

'Hey, John!' He called out.

'Hey, Mick. Where are you headed?' John replied.

'Got to talk to the boss. He's got a big assignment for me.' He kept a cool face.

'Cool. Oh yeah, Chrissie told me to...' Then realization hit him. 'Wait, do you mean what I think you mean? You have a 'big' assignment?'

Mick was grinning from ear to ear. He could not get anything to come out of his mouth, so he just nodded instead.

'Well that's great, man! Well done!' John's enthusiasm sounded genuine, but Mick suspected that John was slightly disappointed he did not get it himself.

'Don't worry, I think he'll make you my second. From what I can see, you're ranked fourth in the U.K., and the two ahead of us are already on missions – one in Hampshire and the other in Scotland.'

'That's wicked! All right, after the meeting, tell me what happened. If he doesn't contact me himself, that is. So I'll go home now and wait for someone to contact me.'

He started to turn around at this point and head for home. But Mick stopped him.

'Hey! What was it you were going to say about Chrissie?'

John stopped and turned around. He fished in his pocket and pulled out a necklace. It was plain except for a small emerald cube on the bottom, with thin silver lines along its edges. Mick felt a large jolt in his stomach as he recognised it with vivid familiarity. It was her favourite necklace.

'She told me to give you this. Something to remind you of her.' John put it into Mick's hands.

'What do you mean? It sounds like she's saying goodbye.' He could not understand. She only lived 5 minutes away.

'Well, she is. Haven't you heard?'

'Heard what?'

'She's moving.'

'Well that's not too...'

'To America.'

There was a pause as Mick digested this information. John eventually broke the silence.

'Why did you give her up, mate? She was really crushed, you know. It just doesn't make sense. She was hot, understanding, kind, and you two really clicked. Why let all that go?'

A memory flashed into Mick's head of a man holding a gun to Christine's head. He just couldn't risk that again. But this had happened before John Corton's time, and he knew nothing of what had happened. Mick owed him the truth. Christine, or Chrissie as her friends called her, went to their school (or Mick's previous school). John was a very good friend of hers.

'I guess I had better tell you the truth.' He walked over to bench and sat down. Then he recounted his tale about why he broke up with Chrissie.

* * *

I shall not tell this tale to you now, for it is a different part of Mick's life, and it is not significant in making him the person who he is known as today. Maybe I'll tell you some when else.

* * *

Mick finished talking. A ringing silence followed. He looked at his watch and realized that he had taken five minutes to tell his story. He was going to be late for his meeting!

'Hey, I've got to go. I'm late in meeting the boss. You know what he's like when people hold him up.'

John snapped out of his thoughts. 'Oh, yeah. That's nasty. Anyway. At least I understand now. Thanks for that. Do you want to go see her? I was thinking of seeing her later anyway. Come with me?'

'Maybe. I'll think about it. But I'll see you later anyway.'

'Yeah, see you.'

The Big Assignment

Mick arrived back at his home five minutes late. He ran upstairs and changed before heading into his 'secret area'. First, he went over to the cupboard and pressed his second and third fingers against the eyes of a poster of Oli Brandon, the famous actor. The eyes glowed red for a second before going out. Then a panel flipped up from behind the name on the poster, with a number code from 1-9 with an 'A' and 'B' below. He punched in the correct code (A1353646). A section of the wall slid up and out of sight.

Mick walked into the fair sized room behind it. He always liked being in this room. It made him feel important. There was a desk with a computer set with camera, printer and a pencil pot on top of it. There were also lots of gadgets round the room on the walls with a conveyer belt protruding from the wall next to the desk.

'Good afternoon, sir.' Said a female voice from the computer. 'The boss is ready and impatient to speak to you.'

'All right! All right! Keep your hair on.' Mick muttered. The computer could never be subtle!

He sat down in front of the desk and turned the monitor of the computer on. There in front of him sat the boss of MI5, just as he would be if he was in the same room as him. He was a clean shaven man and would have been fairly handsome if his hair hadn't started greying so much. Mick didn't usually go in to see him because the boss lived in London and he lived in Reading. It was too risky to head all the way up there and back. And Mick did not really like public transport.

'Hello, Mick. I thought you said half an hour not forty minutes.' The boss said suddenly.

'Sorry, sir,' Mick replied. 'Traffic held me up.' He held the stream of complaints he wanted to say.

'I'm not sure I quite believe you. Anyway, let us not beat about the bush; let us talk about your new 'man'.'

'Sir, can we please stop using the form 'man' when we are face to face. Mick asked. 'Sometimes you confuse me.'

'Alright then, your new assignment.' The boss said huffily. 'You have been given this assignment because it is very near to this new school of yours, so you should be able to go and sneak around without too much trouble.'

'Boss, why are you not just sending in adults, professionals with lots of training, to do the job?

'We've tried,' said the boss with a sigh. 'But every time we send one in there, the moment something big is about to happen, we lose contact. Three times this has happened, and we think a change of strategy would be good.'

'Ok, boss. What do you want me to do?' With a yawn, Mick prepared himself for a long lecture.

'The garage over the road from your new school has had funny goings on. Some of the cars being sent there for repair are just disappearing into thin air. Whenever the owner of the car phones up, the only reply they get is that they have run into some problems and need further time. The most curious thing is that the longest wait is three months and still counting.

Luckily, some of the cars are still coming out. Even so, after some good long drives, the battery packs in. Lately this has been becoming shorter and shorter until after only the third drive, the battery dies.'

'What do you think is happening?' Mick asked. The question was always expected to be asked at some point; it showed a good spy apparently. But Mick did not get that. All it showed was that they listened and obeyed. Was that part of it?

'Well, we have been picking up large waves of energy. The puzzling thing is that we cannot put a finger on what the energy is. My guess is that it has something to do with our new substances for the prisons.' A wince came upon the boss' face.

'How are the prisons going by the way?' Mick queried.

'Ok, I guess. They are a bit behind schedule, but nothing too bad.' Mick guessed otherwise. 'Look for yourself.' The boss changed the screen for a little so as to show one of the CCTV cameras in the most up-to-date prison. He could see all the cool new technology and equipment. He decided to remember it for future reference.

'Who do think is behind it all? Someone we know or someone new?'

'Well,' a grimace appeared across his face this time. 'We are pretty sure it is someone new, but who it is we just do not know.

'Right.' Mick said, thinking that a lie was in there somewhere. He was never sure with his boss. He was always very good at that sort of thing.

He decided not to linger on the subject just yet. 'Is there any back up?'

'Oh yes. You have John Corton. Anyone else you have in mind that you would like? I seem to remember that you liked to work on your own or with a small group; four others at most.'

'Well, there is somebody, but I'm not sure whether they are up to it. Only time will tell, but for the moment, John will do. What about gadgets?'

'John will be happy!' Mick thought.

'Ah, yes. I'd thought you'd bring that up. Well Johnson has looked through all the files and has got some that should do you perfectly. I'll put you onto him now.'

Suddenly the screen changed and a young man dressed very casually in jeans and t-shirt was looking at him.

' 'Ello Mick. 'Ad a good time?' Johnny Johnson was a very friendly guy and was an expert at what he did. But he could get a bit carried away at times. He once built a radar that was really a massive laser!

'Hello, Johnny. What have you got for me this time?'

'You'll enjoy these. Well, we've got ya dis 3-D goggle game which doubles as an x-ray device, an 'eat-detectin' device, an' an electricity-detectin' device. To activate i', ya turn the back ligh' on an' off three times, den select da option ya want. Also, if y'are in a smoke filled room, i' will 'elp you to see through da smoke an' an oxygen mask is part of i', as you can see. The oxygen will last ya 'alf an hour.

We 'ave also got ya a new personal organiser system. We 'ave put all da information ya need on i' and i' 'as an 'idden camera in da back. I' has spy equipment you will find useful loaded onto i', so give time to familiarize yourself with i'. It will also give ya instant contact with us. From da start of da mission there will be someone (*'Or should be,'* Mick thought.) on standby to take your information or calls from da time da mission starts. After dat, you migh' just 'ave to wait.

'Anyway, you also 'ave a torch. This torch 'as an ultra-bright ligh' an' da battery is a smoke bomb wiv a slight sedative in i'. I' will make people feel a lit'le drowsy. Use your gas mask if you set i' off under you. To activate, you just need to press da '+' sign three times.

Lastly, we 'ave your favourite gadget; da shark tooth necklace. Dis shark tooth is really a stun dart. You can use i' if you 'av run ou' of ammo, ya lost ya weapon, summit like dat. Is dat clear?'

'Crystal.' Mick yawned. He was tired.

'Well then. Jus' so's you know; John will get all da same gadgets as you, 'cept his necklace will be a mini explosive. Anyone else 'oo joins your merry band of a man will also be supplied. Anyway, 'ope to see ya round ol' chum.'

'Yeah ok. See you.'

The screen flicked back to the boss.

'Ok, well the school starts in two weeks, so I'll make that the start date. In that time you can come in for a briefing and training on how to handle large assignments. Not that you will pay any attention,' he said in an off-hand manner, 'but it is the regulations. I'm signing off now. Do not forget to tell John.' He was just turning round when he suddenly looked back at the screen.

'Oh, nearly forgot. We need you to have a couple of days to blend in to your role. Give a little time before trying anything. Ok? T.T.F.N.'

'See ya.' Mick switched off the monitor and sighed. What an adventure this was going to be!

The Plan Updated

'Have you seen Mick or John around here lately?' said the boy slash man (who was known as the 'Evil San'), lazily.

'No, sir,' said a fit black man to the San. He had no hair and was very muscular.

'Not at all?' Said the San again. 'Are you sure, Tomodan? Are your men ready and alert 24/7?

'Yes, sir.' Tomodan answered. He was very military and stood at attention all the time. His voice was crisp and sharp. 'We believe that a delay tactic might have been put into operation. Or the job he is taking up hasn't come up to its start date. Neither of them has taken the jobs on offer here. I do not know why though, sir.'

'Is there any job in the area that they could take? We need to know where to find them so that we can kill them quickly.' Said San, standing up. He was getting agitated, and annoyed.

'Not really, sir,' replied Tomodan, 'there are a couple of jobs on offer at the shop, one at the pub, and there is about half a dozen at the garage just up the road. They would not be able to work in the pub because they would not be old enough.'

'Yes, yes. And the same would be said about the BP jobs. We have to assume the shops. You know what to do.' The San sat back down. Tomodan still stood there, though. He cleared his throat and continued with his ideas.

'I did have another thought, sir. There are places in the school about half a mile away, but that is not important. What is, though, is that there is a completely new school starting just down the road, behind the business centre. Earlier this morning there was unusual activity happening there.'

The San stood back up.

'Oh yes. And what was that?'

'It was the sound of bullet shots and a lot of cars. I believe these boys are joining the school. This would explain the delay. Also, a terrorist plot set up by the great Himo D.I. Karagammaro, your master, was meant to be carried out today. You can work the rest out for yourself.'

'I see what you're getting at, Tomodan.' The San thoughtfully said. 'Get all men on alert for when that school starts, and try to cause him pain. His main hurt is seeing innocent people suffering, especially people he likes. Girls generally tend to favour him since any girl usually likes a strong, cool, and handsome guy. Try capturing one that is close to him. That will cause him pain. Then you can kill him. I want revenge for the pain he caused me. You can go now.'

'Yes, sir.'

Tomodan left the room, leaving the San to ponder on what he had heard. Mick wasn't really a lady's man, but he was quite a hit with them. When they realize what he does, they all come clamouring over themselves for him. But he wasn't going to give them that chance; not by a long shot.

The First Day at School

One month later, Mick awoke in his room, completely awake and alert. For a moment he could not remember what was special about this particular day, but then he remembered; it was his first day at his new school! He jumped out of bed and was ready by the door three quarters of an hour later. He was excited to see what it would be like, see who had got in, and because it was the first day of his assignment; probably the easiest part, settling in. The school (called Greater Reading Comprehensive) started at 8:45, and Mick arrived there with plenty of time to spare.

Only the head had arrived. As he went in, he found not many desks set out. The head explained that since they had only just started (and there weren't many schools that were full anyway) there was only about 50 students coming. Since there was so few, they would have only a few groups. They were Infants, Lower Juniors, Upper Juniors, and Senior School.

During that day Mick got to know everyone vaguely, including the teachers. He got to know his group (Senior School) better, though. The head was in charge of this group. There was an Indian boy one year older than himself and his brother who was 16. There was Katrina and her sister, Ana. There was the son of the head who was 16 and was called Ryan. And there was himself.

They were all very friendly and hard working, so it was easy for them to get on with their work since they respected each other's need to learn. The next couple of days went without hitches, except the fact that during Tuesday afternoon's work, they had a power cut.

There was one hiccup, however, that scared Mick. While the class was being told how to take a tests abiding to the set regulations, something distracted Mick from outside the window. What he saw was a man trying to get into the building. He kept on trying, ignoring the doorbell, and tried to get in; in what seemed like a secretive way.

'Mick, please pay attention. This is important.' The head scorned. 'Why are you looking out of the window?'

'Oh, sorry miss.' Mick replied. 'I just think someone is trying to break into the school. Come and look.'

Everyone made their way to the window. Everyone was intrigued at the funny man who seemed to now be trying to pick the lock; but very unsuccessfully. The head opened the window and called for the man to come and speak to her.

As he came, he seemed a little on edge.

'Hello. Is there anything I can do for you?' The head asked.

'Ummm, yes, there is.' The strange man asked. 'I'm trying to find a Mick Denning; do you know where I could find him?

'I'm right here. What do you want?' Mick said.

'Oh, ok.' Something like surprise or shock crossed the man's face for a second, but he controlled it and reached into his jacket and pulled out a letter.

'A man came up to me in the street; a complete stranger, telling me to give this letter to a Mick Denning and that he could be found at the Greater

Reading Comprehensive.' Mick took the letter from the man, but he still held on.

'This man told me to take the advice given.'

As he said it, an evil look came to his eye. For some reason, Mick didn't quite believe the part of his story about receiving the letter from a stranger. He finally let go of it and walked off, putting on a hat at a jaunty angle.

'What a strange fellow he was.' The head said, and she continued with her talk.

At the end of the day, Mick went into the toilets and opened the letter he had been given.

It read:

Dear Mr. Denning and Mr. Corton,

I hope you realize that this job you have been given is to your heart's content. Unfortunately, it has given you some dangerous enemies. I hope you realize this, for it would be dangerous for you not to. Yes, I know about your little assignment. For Mr. Denning, I warn you; get out of my territory. And Mr. Corton, give up and go home.

Lastly, a little advice. If you know what is good for you, get lost while you have a chance. If you do not, you'll pay for it; badly. You have till tomorrow at noon to hear your reply, spies without codenames!

Yours threateningly,

Consequences

Mick had been shocked by the letter, but he had also experienced a sense of excitement. Mick felt as if he was getting underway with his big assignment at last. The next day, Thursday, Mick appeared at school as usual, but by bike; he needed the exercise because an injury had put him out of action for about 4 months last year.

As he arrived at the school, a man standing just outside the garage opposite the school took off his glasses and stared at him. He then turned round and quickly walked inside the building. Mick felt a growing sense of unease coming upon him. Just at that moment, Katrina turned up, with the rest of her family coming round the corner behind her.

'Something the matter?' She queried.

'Oh no, nothing in particular.' Mick replied, 'Just a growing unease. What lessons do we have today?

'Well, we have the morning period of study, and then break. After that it's practical work until lunch, and after that it's games up at the park.'

'Cool. Let's go inside. I'm starting to feel cold.' The reason for the coldness was that the man from the garage had come back out and he might have just heard that they would be going to the park for their games lesson after lunch. The unease rapidly increased.

The day went well but Mick's unease didn't lessen. When the time to go to games arrived, Mick was positively terrified at what would happen. It didn't help that he wasn't relatively good with surprises, either. Mick was on edge all the way up to the park. They reached the park which was up the hill near the school. The lesson started and, since Mick didn't notice anything amiss, let his troubles lessen and started to enjoy the lesson.

The last game of the day was a game of Rounders and Mick was up for batting. Katrina was in his team and was at second base and another younger girl at third base. The bowler threw the ball with a lot of fall so Mick hit the ball hard and it went high and far, with about two people chasing after it. Mick ran as fast as he could along with the other two girls. Katrina and the other girl reached the fourth base at practically the same time. By that time Mick had reached the third base. Even after the bad injury, he was still fit and could run fast and for long distances.

Suddenly, Mick felt very scared. He had just seen the bush down one side of the park rustle; and there was no wind to speak of at that time. Just as Mick passed the fourth base, he felt a prickling on the back of his neck. He almost heard a buzzing in the air around him warning about the incoming danger. He had been trained to act on this sixth sense and so he followed instincts. He jumped so his body was parallel with the ground. As he did, he heard a bang from the bush and felt the air move beneath him. The bullet had missed him by about a centimetre.

But it had hit Katrina.

As Mick turned around, he saw Katrina on her knees with her right leg bleeding from just above the knee. She looked to be in serious pain.

'Mick, help me!' She gasped.

Mick was usually a calm and collected boy. He wasn't one to get angry easily or fight needlessly. But seeing an innocent person injured for no reason really got him angry. The fact that he was the reason the assassin was there did not help either.

With his eyes ablaze, Mick charged at the figure that had just emerged from the bush. Luckily for Mick, the gun he had used was a low power hand gun, and he had had to reload. Mick ran as fast as he could and charged straight into the man's abdomen. The man staggered backwards, slightly winded. Mick hadn't done himself any good either, since he was at a loss of what to do next. So he got into his basic fighting stance and waited for the gunman to make his move. Not a good idea.

Once the gunman had recovered, he also got into a basic fighting stance, but drew a knife from his belt. The man ran at Mick and sliced at his throat. But Mick grabbed his arm and blocked the punch for his stomach. The man, being a good two heads taller than Mick, now towered over him. And, since his arms were still held by Mick, he drove him backwards into a thorn bush, giving Mick cuts all over. Mick pushed him away, letting the man regain control of his knife. This time he advanced on Mick in a more professional approach. He stepped forward and then half a step back, all the time jabbing and slashing with his knife.

Mick had to get that knife off of him. The only hope he had was to get him off balance and knock him out while he had the chance. So he methodically dodged his attacks and worked around him, trying to find a chance at getting the man off balance. At last it came.

The man had brought his arm up high and about to slash down. Mick dropped and swung his leg at the man; not enough to trip him up, but enough to put him off balance. The man stumbled backwards as one leg was taken from underneath him. Unfortunately for Mick, the knife arm came down anyway. As Mick straightened up, the knife came down, with the point just catching him on the lip. It stung, but Mick ignored it and brought a stunning blow to the man's wrist, making him drop the knife. Mick picked it up and tried stabbing and slashing with it. He kicked the man in the chest and caused him to take a step back. Mick then jumped up as high as he could, and brought the knife handle swinging down to crash into the man's temple like a cosh, knocking him out cold.

Mick walked as fast as he could back to the group from the school that had congregated around Katrina. They looked anxious.

'Get out the way! Let me through!' Mick yelled. He looked at Katrina who was now lying on the ground. She looked in pain, but in reality it was not a bad wound; she had not lost much blood and the bullet had not gone in far and had come out. Obviously it had only skimmed her leg.

'Do you feel ok?' Mick asked.

'I think so, but I feel a bit ill.'

'Ok. I just need to get you to school.'

"You can carry on with the lesson now. I'm fine." Mick told the rest of the class. So they went back to the games lesson (kids were known to get into trouble and it was best to let them get on with it themselves; it helped them grow up). The teacher was not so sure, but could not leave the other kids.

'Can you walk? It would be a lot easier and safer.'

'I don't know. I can have a go though.'

'Good. If I can get you back to school, you'll feel a lot more comfortable. Here, I'll help you up.'

Mick pulled Katrina up and supported her whilst she steadied herself.

'I feel fine, except for the pain in my leg. I feel a bit dizzy too.'

'That would just be because of standing up too quickly after lying down. Probably should have let you do it a little slower.'

Katrina let out a small gasp. 'Oh, my dratted leg; it's still bleeding!'

'I can deal with that.' Mick tore off the arm of his shirt and wrapped it tightly round her leg, just below the knee, with a bit of end material covering the wound. Finally they were ready. Mick let Katrina go at her own pace. He eventually overtook her so if anyone bad did come up the hill, he could protect her and sort them out at his will.

They travelled down the hill at a good pace. Mick suddenly felt uneasy again. Great, more trouble. Half way down the hill there were road works, with the section of path next to it bordered off. On the grass next to it though was a bench. Mick jumped up to run along the bench. It saved getting his trainers muddier than they already were.

As Mick's first foot touched the bench, his other foot got hit by a sudden force and sent him flying off the bench. He landed flat on the ground. He crawled as fast as he could to a van that had parked just behind the road works.

'Mick, are you ok? What happened?' Mick had forgotten all about Katrina. She had come running up to see what had happened.

'I'm fine. But you shouldn't be running.' He replied. He looked at his shoe. A section of the heel's rubber had been ripped away, obviously because a bullet had hit it. Mick quickly looked out the window of the van to try and see his opponent. The window shattered, spraying them with glass. It had not been in vain though. He had seen his opponent standing with a handgun on the opposite pavement. Mick could see how poor these men were since he could handle them with ease.

Mick reached for his waist, where his long-forgotten Beretta 92FS was hiding. He drew it out and from under the van shot a thin needle right into the man's leg and he crumpled out cold.

A New Recruit

Mick walked, or slightly hobbled, to the bottom of the hill (the bullet had slightly caught the bottom of his foot making it painful to walk on). Once he had checked that it was safe, they sat done on a bench to rest.

'How stupid am I!' Mick yelled at himself. 'I should have paid attention in my lesson. *'Always two there are.'* I should have known. I am such a dimwit!' Mick kept ranting on at himself like this for several minutes, until Katrina had had enough.

'Will you shut up?! Stop putting yourself down, it doesn't help you. Just take in what happened and move on. Learn from it. You can't change the past. So just shut up!'

Mick responded to her outburst with silence.

'Mick?' Katrina said.

'Yeah.'

'Well I've noticed that where you are, trouble is. First, the attack on my interview. I nearly got killed! Then that strange man trying to break into the school. Lastly, today. Twice you have been attacked and I have got hurt.'

'Sounds as if you wanted to get hurt. Maybe to impress me?' Mick muttered to himself.

'Oh, shut up and listen.' However Mick thought he saw Katrina blush a little.

'What I want to know is, who are you? Why are you surrounded by danger? Why is a teenager with a gun fighting adults with many lethal weapons?'

Well, you won't believe me.'

Give me your best shot.' Katrina folded her arms and looked confident.

'Ok. Here it goes. I'm a spy for the government. I work in the department of S.P.F.T. That stands for Spy Police For Teenagers, so we can spy, but are in contact with the police and can command some of the lower ranking policemen. The people at the interview were terrorists who were trying to crash an airplane into Big Ben so it would fall onto the Houses of Parliament and kill everyone inside. I stopped it.

The person who handed me the letter was, in a sense, the cause of the people attacking me today. The letter that I got yesterday told me to quit my latest mission, or they will kill me. The people today were sent because I didn't give up my mission.

The worse thing is, more will be coming. They were probably the worst assassins. Better ones will be sent, and eventually, I probably won't stand a chance. Well, what do you think?'

Katrina had not moved from when she folded her arms. Only now did she move, but it was only her lips.

'I think that makes perfect sense. Why else would those men be chasing you? But one last question. I think what you do is really cool. I would like to learn to so; can I be a spy too?'

It was Mick who was surprised this time.

'What did you say?'

'I said, "Can you get me a job to become a spy?"'

Mick was stunned.

'Well, I guess I could try. Are you sure you really want to. I never thought anyone, especially you... no offence,' Katrina had looked offended, '...

would ask me anything like that again. But I can try, yeah.'

'What do you mean, again?' Katrina looked puzzled and had a suspicion that she was not the only one to ask that question to Mick.

'There was another boy called John Corton who asked me the same question. He was in a drama lesson at his new drama school when some people came and attacked his teacher, who was a spy. His teacher was overwhelmed, but not before he had hit his panic button. I was the closest spy to him that wasn't already active. I arrived there and got him free, but the men who had captured him saw me, so we fought them off. John saw me and asked what was going on. I think you can tell what happened next.'

'Right...' Katrina looked a very distant. She did not really hear Mick when he asked her whether she was ready to go back to school. She came out of her day-dreaming when a boy about their age came powering up to them on roller skates at a terrific speed - way beyond normal human capabilities.

'You alright?' Said this new boy. He had black towsly hair and narrow eyes, but looked very fit. Anxious, too, she noticed.

'Yeah, we're fine,' Mick answered. 'Katrina got a bullet in the leg, though. I didn't hit the panic button, did I?'

'You must have done it by accident. I got a first aid kit here. Would you like me to patch that leg up for you?'

'Yeah, but who are you? And how did you just do that?' Katrina was a bit shocked. She had a feeling she knew who it was, but didn't like to guess, just in case.

'Sorry, I didn't introduce you.' Mick said apologetically. 'Katrina, this is John Corton. John, this is Katrina Baker. We were just talking about you, John.'

'Oh, really?!' John said, surprised, as he started on Katrina's wound.

Mick explained everything they had missed both of them and then left them to themselves as he pondered how to approach the boss about a new recruit. Especially with it being a girl.

How to Work Round a Boss

At the end of the day, Mick went home and did all the homework that he had been set. Since he was a clever kid, he completed it in half an hour.

Then he walked to his cupboard, placed his fingers on the eyes and typed in the code. He was ready.

'Good morning, sir,' the female voice said. 'What do you wish to do?

'Get in contact with the boss. I need to speak to him about an urgent matter.'

'Anything else he needs to know?'

'Yes. Just tell him it's a matter concerning recruits.'

'As you wish, sir.' Mick sat down as he waited for the boss to get back to him. He was still nervous, even though during his homework, he had found a way he thought he could persuade the boss.

What concerned Mick most was that the boss didn't always agree to the choices some of his men made. He got angry (a rare occurrence) when one spy tried to sneak his girlfriend in to be a cook. The boss hadn't liked the idea, but even more than that, he didn't like the idea that it was a woman. He thought of women as if they needed protecting, and they could not do it themselves. He was wrong though. Some girls he had met were pretty tough. Katrina didn't seem like that kind of person. But, then again he hadn't seen her fight. He didn't even know if she could fight. Mick had a sense of foreboding as the monitor flickered into life and the boss sat there, not looking his best.

'Well, Mick. I think I know what you've called me for, thanks to the hint. Who is it this time?'

The boss' face went hard. Mick got the lump in his throat cleared and started his narrative of what had happened that day up to when they stopped at the bench. The bosses face had softened, but still was not completely relaxed.

'So far you have only given me a report of the day's events. Stop beating about the bush and get on with this recruiting!' The boss was nearly shouting now.

'Well, this girl I was taking to treat started to feel tired as we reached the bottom of the hill. We sat down on a bench and rested a bit. I got angry at myself and she shut me up. She then asked if...' he trailed off.

'She asked whether she could join us, is that it?' He didn't look happy now. Mick sat back in his chair, resigned. The boss would never allow a girl of Katrina's age join them, unless she could prove herself worthy. Mick suddenly had a new plan in his mind. He sat up, with a forked tongue of honey.

'I know, sir, that you don't like girls in this organization. You think it is too dangerous for them.'

'Yes, it is.' The boss looked sullen; the perfect time to bite.

'Well, sir. I have had an idea. What if she could prove herself to you?'

'What do you mean? If you mean she comes in here and has a couple of fights with some of our guys, that just is not good enough. Good idea, though. Nearly caught me.

I mean, if she can easily do all the requirements we have to pass to become a spy, would that not mean she was capable?'

The boss was starting to give in and was struggling to find excuses to stop Katrina from joining.

'Well, yes, but…'

'You can't say no when us boys can get in after passing the tests. When a girl takes it though and she passes the test and you will refuse her, what will people think of you then, eh?' Mick was getting to the boss. He was failing; Mick could see it. The boss looked at his desk thinking, his head twitching from side to side trying to find a way out…

'Alright, you win. She can come in tomorrow and take the tests. But she **must** get above 60% to get in. Her results will be in by Saturday. Goodbye.'

The screen went blank.

Results

That Saturday, Mick arranged for the Bakers to come round his house for lunch. This gave him the perfect opportunity for Katrina to get her results.

At 1:00, the Denning's started to get ready. They needed the house to be tidy (which it already was) but Mick's mum was very picky about that sort of thing, so they still had to make sure everything was spick and span whilst the she cooked the lunch. The Bakers were due at 1:30 so they had plenty of time.

* * *

At 1:40 the bell rang and Mick went to open it. As he opened the door he got a sudden shock.

Katrina was standing there, looking her very best. Mick saw all her make-up put on to perfection and her choice of clothes; a short sleeve t-shirt with a shirt over the top with a leather mini skirt. A lump came to Mick's throat as he looked at her.

'Err, hi,' he eventually managed to get out.

'Hi, when are the results going to be here?'

'Is that all you can think about?' Mick gave a small chuckle. 'Come on in. My friend, Chrissie, should be in the living room. She was just about to leave, but you could go say hi. She is leaving for America tomorrow, so don't become too good friends.'

'Alright. Sounds like a good idea. I had better get to know some of your friends.'

She walked off towards the living room. Mick watched her go, and as she did he gave a low whistle.

'You got a crush on her or something?'

Harry had just reached the door. Mick had become good friends with Harry, and they easily had fun playing games together.

'Yeah right, as if. Hey Ana; Hey Lucy.'

'Hello, Mick. How are you?'

'I'm fine. You go on in to the living room. I'll wait for Daniel.'

Daniel came in a few moments later with the baby. They both went into the living room.

His living room was modest, but had a good sense of style. Katrina and Chrissie were talking animatedly to each other as if they were childhood friends. So Mick sat back and talked with Harry. Mick's dad was talking to Daniel and Ana had joined Katrina and Chrissie. Everything was just fine.

Harry stopped talking for a second or two, and then said, 'Can I play on your XBOX unlimited degrees?'

'Sure thing. It's upstairs in my room. Follow me.'

As they got up, Chrissie piped up. 'I had probably better go. I said I would be home by two.'

'Oh, ok.' Mick was feeling a bit awkward. 'I'll see you out.' Chrissie walked past him heading to the door. As she did, Mick got a good smell of her hair. It smelled of cherry, as it always did. He felt a massive churn in the pit of his stomach and remembered what John had said:

'*She was really gutted, you know.*'

He pushed it out of his mind as they reached the door and he opened it for her.

'Well. I guess this is goodbye,' Chrissie said.

'Yeah, I guess it is.' Mick kept his eyes on his feet. He couldn't look at her. It would be too difficult.

'I hope things go well for you.' Chrissie was finding it a little difficult as well.

'Yeah. You too. I hope the plane journey is ok. Thanks for the necklace.' There was a pause. 'Well, goodbye then.' He held out his hand. He still did not look at her.

Chrissie looked at the hand, but did not take it. She reached up and tipped Mick's face up to look at her.

'Just say it.' She said sadly.

'Say what?' A lump had again come to Mick's throat, so it came out hoarsely.

'You'll miss me.'

Mick looked intensely into her eyes, and saw the pain he had caused her. Not just by being a spy, but with breaking up with her. Mick felt really guilty. He pulled her into a passionate hug, which was returned just as fiercely.

'I'll miss you. And I'm sorry.' Mick whispered into her ear. No explanation was needed. Mick's eyes started to well up with tears.

But a noise to his left caused him to look over. Katrina and Harry stood there watching them.

Mick cleared his throat and pulled away. Chrissie saw why immediately.

'Um, well, see you.' Chrissie walked out of the door. Mick watched her go as he closed the door. That chapter of his life was over. He just wished it had not of been so painful.

Katrina came up behind him with a curious look.

'What was that between you two?' She sounded confused, but almost seemed a little jealous.

'Nothing you need to know. How did you two get on anyway?' He tried to make it sound as if it was unimportant, but failed miserably.

'Oh, we got on great! I have her number so we can keep in touch. She seemed really nice.' Katrina put on a sly look. 'It would be difficult for a guy to not want to go out with her.' She walked up the stairs after Harry, while Mick hid a horrified expression.

All 3 of them went up to Mick's bedroom and had a good time playing on his game station. At last, Harry got up to see his parents. This left Mick and Katrina alone.

'This is our chance.'

'Let's go for it.'

Mick got up, walked to his poster and did the usual codes. They both went into his secret room, Katrina filled with awe.

Mick sat down at the desk. The P.C. turned on almost as soon as he sat down (he had had the computer programmed as such). Right in front of them was a grumpy head of MI5.

'Hello, boss. This is Katrina; I don't think you've met.'

Mick pulled up a seat for Katrina and she sat down on the edge of it nervously.

'So, there is no point beating about the bush, Katrina in your test, you scored 79%. This means that you are in. You had some training yesterday, and soon we will be putting you through a test to see how far you have come. For now that is it. Goodbye and well done.'

The monitor flickered off.

Katrina jumped off her seat and started whooping. Eventually she calmed down, but her hair was now everywhere and she looked a total mess. Mick started to laugh but tried to keep it down. Even so, he could not stop a grin spreading all over his face.

'What?'

Katrina had noticed him and was looking at him puzzled, but still in a joyful mood.

'Nothing, nothing.' But the grin still didn't go away.

'What?'

'Nothing. Really! Come on, I am sure lunch will be ready soon.'

They both went downstairs to find everyone getting up to go to lunch.

'*What exquisite timing.*' Mick thought.

A Trap

When they were all seated at the table, Mick's dad poured out the drinks. There were two bottles of Schloer that Mick did not think his parents had bought, so he assumed that the Bakers had brought them. Ana was sitting next to him so he asked,

'Did you bring the 2 Schloer bottles with you?

'No, we only brought one with us. That's the red one on the table. I have never seen the white. Didn't you buy it?'

'No, that's why I am worried.' Mick answered through gritted teeth, because his dad had just handed round the white and the adults had just held a toast, but the children had not. The adults suddenly fainted and fell asleep in their seats. Mick knew immediately that they were all in danger, and that they couldn't stay in the house. He immediately took control.

'Ok everyone. It is certain that someone is after us. I don't know why, but it is not safe to stay here anymore and we all need to split up for safety. Okay, Ana, Harry, and Katrina; you all need to go to a friend's house for now.'

'Not me,' butted in Katrina, 'I'm going home.'

'Ok, but you lot still need to go to a friend's house. We'll all go together. I'll go to John's house just down the road.

'All understand? Let's get moving then!'

* * *

By the end of the day, everyone was in a house - except for Mick. John had his grandparents round, so he didn't have room for Mick. He knew he couldn't go back home; on his handheld he had seen on the security cameras three men break into the house.

The only other place he could go was his old friend Gareth Hunsan. He always had room. They were old friends with an inactive relationship. They would see each other every so often at one another's house, but they had really only seen each other at school. Gareth had gone to the same primary school as John and himself, but he had gone to a different secondary school, putting their friendship at an even greater distance. They had not seen each other properly for over three years.

Mick got to his house to find that Gareth was out at a friend's house for a sleep over, but his mother still allowed him to stay the night.

* * *

Mick awoke next morning. He had slept well since he done a lot of exercise the day before getting Harry and Ana to safety at friends houses. He was going to need it as a lot was going to happen that day, though he did not know it.

Mick had breakfast and then decided to take a walk. He went upstairs to get his shoes. He got up and sat on the only seat in the room; a high seat right next to a low shelf full of books.

As he did the laces up, his hand slipped and hit a book off the shelf. It started to fall, but was caught before the final corner could come off. He looked closer and saw that it had been caught on a hinge and was connected electronically to something.

Mick heard a humming noise and he looked round to see where the noise was coming from. As he did, a section of wall slid back to reveal a room with a desk in the centre and lots of buttons and switches along the wall. Mick went inside. He didn't press any buttons (it was too risky since none of them were labelled), but looked at what was on the desk. There on the desk sat some equipment that looked oddly familiar, as if he had once seen it from a distance. He ran and got his P.O. out and took pictures of all the equipment and the room itself. Then he sent it all to the boss with a message saying,

'Do you know what this stuff is? Found it in a friend's house. Doesn't feel right.'

He also sent a copy to John and also to Katrina. With the last letter he added,

'Coming to see you. Be on the look-out in case I am followed.'

Mick felt uneasy. And when he felt uneasy, something bad nearly always happened (as we have seen already). He decided to leave straight away. He righted the book on the shelf, which closed the door. Michael grabbed the one rucksack he had brought with him, packed it, and left the house. He ran down a few streets; left, left again, straight ahead, now right.

Eventually he reached the J11. Katrina lived just over the motorway from the school; Katrina's house was one of the safest places he could think of without having to travel far. He kept on running. He was a good long distance runner at school.

Mick finally reached sight of her house, and ran into trouble.

'Trouble' was 20 men all armed with bats, steel pipes and clubs waiting for him. They were very muscly and strong; it would take a little while for his gun needles to take effect in those thick skins.

They didn't say anything, but they just charged at him with aggression. Mick got out his gun and fired three shots at them, each with three needles in. Seven people fell, but only momentarily. In moments they were up and charging again, but sluggishly.

Mick turned his gun over so he was holding the muzzle and started using it to block incoming attacks and as a cosh. It was rather effective. 5 people fell under the gun, but a particularly wild stroke from a steel bar took it from his hands. It went skidding away and settled in the curb.

As good as he was, Mick couldn't stand the force from the 8 remaining men (the men he had shot at the beginning had finally gone down). He got hit over and over with bats, clubs, and fists. He was easily hurt because, even though he was strong, he was still young.

Eventually it became too much for him and he collapsed on the floor in a heap, near to losing consciousness. He had a badly cut arm, and he thought he might have cracked his skull; blood dripped from his hair. The rest of his body was drained of all strength.

'*I'll be a walking bruise and scar museum if I survive this,*' Mick thought to himself.

More of the men had finally gone down, leaving 5 to tower over him as they prepared to finished him off. Before they could however, Mick asked huskily, 'Why did you attack me? Why did you attack an innocent boy like me?'

'Innocent?!' The man who must have been the leader had a high voice with plenty of malice in it. He was taunting Mick even to the end.

'Innocent?!' He said again. 'We know what you did. You...'

FLUMPH!!!

Two of the men circling Mick fell backwards and landed flat on their backs. The leader turned round.

'You two, go look around. See who is there. I'll cover the kid. The Master said to bring him alive to him personally.'

The two men walked off to search the bushes on the edge of the road. Mick felt comforted though; they were not going to kill him, and someone was helping him.

As they stepped onto the curb, one fell flat on his face, and fell silent. The other ducked down immediately, sensing the danger. He crept forward, making sure he had balance all the time, but...

WHAM!!!

A foot came out of nowhere to smash into the man's face. He was out cold in seconds, because out the bushes leapt Katrina, with her hand coming to grip him in the neck and attack the pressure point.

Katrina walked off the curb, picked up Mick's gun and turned it onto the leader and last remaining man. Mick used up all his remaining energy to swing his legs into the back of the man's knees. The man fell down cringing.

'Please don't shoot me! I don't want to die.'

'Oh, you won't die.' Mick said in a rasping voice. 'You'll just be knocked out for a couple of hours. Just answer me this. Who is this Master?'

But the man did not answer.

'Fine. Shoot him.' Mick was in an impatient mood.

Katrina shot him. Then she ran over to him.

'Are you all right? What should I do? I'll go get help!'

'Katrina...'

'No, I'll stay and try to help you. Do you have a phone? You need a paramedic.'

'Katrina, just...'

'Where are you hurt? Just show me so I can help.'

'Katrina, just calm down!'

Finally she stopped nattering. She stopped talking and started to listen to Mick.

'Just get me to your house. Get some neighbours to help you carry me. Then just patch me up. Don't call for a paramedic, just a doctor. Hospital is the first place they will look.' Mick's sight started to waver. 'I'm going to pass out soon, so do what I say and do it quickly; they'll be onto us pretty quick. Once we're in your house we'll be sa... Once we get there we will... we will be...'

And he finally passed out.

The Siege of Baker's House

Mick woke up. He hurt all over. Even his eyes hurt when he tried to open them. He kept them closed.

He tried to remember what had happened the day before... Or was it only a few hours ago? He did not know. His mind wasn't working. It was taking forever for his thoughts to mean anything. But suddenly everything came back to him in a rush. He sat bolt upright and opened his eyes in fright...

Or, at least he tried to. His back was very sore and as he tried to move it he found it to be aching. His eyes opened slightly with a crackling; his eyelashes were coated with blood.

He groaned. Suddenly a voice came, but it sounded quiet and far away. The words were slow reaching his head and they did not make any sense. But eventually it came to him.

'Oh, you are awake. Good! I was starting to get really worried!'

Mick recognized the voice as Katrina's. He made an effort and his eyelashes came unstuck. There she was, kneeling beside him, a look of relief on her face.

Mick took in his surroundings. He was lying on a sofa in a fairly large, and highly decorated room. The room was nice magnolia colour, with the furniture all the same colour. There were flowery borders on the walls, and many pictures dotted the place. The sofa he was on by the door. Three other chairs sat in the corners of the room. A TV and a hi-fi system sat by the electric fire, nearly opposite the door.

Mick brought his attention back to Katrina as she started to talk again.

'I really thought that you had done yourself in, but the doctor and I brought you back. It was tough, I can tell you. But we did it!'

A smile came onto her face.

'Do you want a drink? Or something to eat?'

As Mick thought about it he was extremely hungry, not to mention thirsty.

'Yes, please. I really am tired but I do need something to eat and drink.'

Mick started to get up, but Katrina stopped him.

'Not so fast, mate. I'll get you your dinner.' (For so it was, since he had missed lunch and it was now 6.00, but Mick did not know that at the present).

'You can stay there and rest. You have a badly bashed skull, bruises everywhere, and a tooth missing. You need to regain every inch of strength you can, doctor's orders. He's gone now, but what he said still applies.'

Katrina got up to go get his dinner, and it was only then that he noticed that Katrina was wearing a dressing gown. This and the mention of dinner gave Mick the suspicion that it was very late, since he did not go to bed until 9.00, and he was sure Katrina went to bed no earlier.

'What's the time? It must be late.' Katrina had just reached the door and turned round. Mick motioned to her clothing. She looked down, and as she looked up she was blushing slightly.

'Not really. It is only 6.00. As to my dressing gown, I've just had a shower and I stayed down here since there was no point in getting changed until I went to bed.' She rushed out the room.

Mick looked round and saw a clock on the mantelpiece. It read 6.05.

'*Close enough.*' He thought.

Now that he wasn't talking, he had time to reflect on what had happened that morning. Was it really that short time ago? It felt like a month!

He thought back to the secret room. How stupid it was of him not to think of a laser trip wire! But what bothered him the most was the secrecy of the room. Lots of young boys had secret rooms, it was the in thing. But all of them were fantastical, usually with themes of their favourite movies, or where they could hide things.

But never had Mick seen any quite so business-like (apart from his own, of course!) or peculiar. He knew Gareth had lots of secrets to hide, many more than a usual kid, but he wasn't as formal as all that!

Or was he?

That reminded him of the equipment he had seen and the information he had sent to MI5. He wondered whether they had replied.

At that moment Katrina walked in carrying a tray with some food and drink on it.

'Thanks a lot, Katrina.' She handed the tray over and he started to eat. Katrina sat down on the floor beside the sofa and hugged her legs whilst he finished.

When he had Mick asked her where his gadgets were.

'Here they are,' she said as she brought them to him. Mick picked up the P.O. and turned it on.

He had three messages. The first was a reply from Katrina and the second a reply from John. The third message got him annoyed.

It was only an automatic reply from MI5.

Mick did the only thing he could; he re-sent the message twice. If the computer received the same message from the same person three times, it put the message on 'urgent' status and is sent to the top of the list.

Mick had just closed the flap when it vibrated, meaning it had received a message. He re-opened it and read. What he saw made him so annoyed he nearly overturned his dinner.

The message read,

ERROR!!!
MESSAGE FAILED!!!
DAMAGE TO ANTENNA AND CAN NO LONGER TRANSMIT OR RECIEVE MESSAGES.

During the fight, the antenna must have been hit. This now meant that Mick would have to go back home to get the message through.

Katrina got up and looked over his shoulder.

'That must be annoying. Were you expecting anything? Was John meant to contact you?'

'No,' Mick replied. 'I'll have to tell you the whole story anyway, so you might as well hear it now. It will explain a lot of things that you don't know.'

So Mick started his story. Katrina turned her back to him, sat down, and rested her head on the edge of the sofa. Mick could tell she had been telling the truth about having a shower; her hair was still slightly damp.

For the next hour they sat there discussing and contemplating the problem that had appeared; what should they do? Katrina's house had been fitted with the simple defences, but it had not quite been equipped with communication equipment, so they were in a jam. Neither did either of them have the phone number so they could not just use a phone. No safe place to go and no possible way of letting anyone know of their predicament.

They got so wound up in their conversation that they did not see the time trickle by. But even so, they kept on talking.

'So, what did you do whilst I was going through hell, then?' Mick asked.

'Well, I arrived here without any trouble, but I ran into a spot of bother when I went shopping for food. Somebody saw me walking into the shop, so they decided to ambush me as I left. Three men tried to grab me, but I swung the bag into one of the men's' faces and I ran back into the shop. They tried to follow me, but the shop's security guards were too much for them. They confessed that they were part of the group who drugged our parents and told me of a plot to kill you. John also.

That is how I came to help you. I was on the look-out because I knew if you had trouble, this was one of the places you most likely to turn to.'

'And I was right!' She had a jubilant expression on her face.

'Well thanks. You saved my life, and I've saved yours. We're square.'

'Yeah.'

'What's the time?' Mick couldn't see the clock face since it had become dark and the only light was coming from the hall.

Katrina got up and walked over to the clock.

'Man!' She exclaimed. 'It's half past eight! You ought to be getting some rest. The doctor said you should get to bed by eight. You're half an hour late already.'

Mick started to laugh.

'Katrina, stop being so fussy! You sound like someone's mother! I'm feeling fine.'

Mick tried to sit himself up, but his back started to throb and ache with as much ferocity as before. He lay back down with a groan.

'See what I mean?' Katrina retorted with a look. 'Now, do you need anything?'

'Yes, could I have a pillow please?'

'Oh, sure!'

Katrina ran off and came back with a pillow. When she got back she found Mick with a doggy pout expression.

'Auntie Katrina?'

'What?' She answered cautiously.

'Can you tell me a bed time story? Afterwards can you tuck me in?'

'Oi!'

Katrina flung the pillow into his face.

'All right! All right!' Mick flung his hands up in mock surrender.

'Good. Well, night then.' Katrina said. After a pause, she added, 'Um, Mick?'

'Yes.'

'I wanted to tell you that well... um... I just wanted to say... oh, just forget it.' And with that she ran out of the room.

Mick put his tray down on the floor and made himself as comfortable as he could.

What on earth was all that about? Well, he would just have to wait till the morning to ask.

But the next morning, many things would drive that thought completely from his mind.

* * *

Next morning, Mick was awoken early. At first he could not realize what had woken him. He looked round to see if Katrina had woken him up, but she was nowhere to be seen. Then Mick heard it. It was the dustbin van. He could hear the pistons working as they picked up the dustbins. He settled back down as he listened to it going up the road and then reversing back with usual hum.

But wait a minute, only the usual hum? Where was the warning that they played when it was reversing?

Mick got up slowly and stiffly and looked out of the window. There was the van alright. It was reversing towards the house. Coming down the road also (driving forwards however) were two normal vans. Then the most unlikely thing possible happened. The dustbin van and the two other vans stopped right outside the house! Then men jumped out and set up a road block. They were blocking the house in.

On the side of one of the vans was a sign. Mick strained to see it, and eventually worked it out.

It read,

The Evil San

Mick was astonished. How did the Evil San known where he was? Was the gang he had met earlier in league with him? What was going on? Mick started to pull himself together. He tidied himself up as much as he could, then went to wake Katrina.

Mick was a man of courtesy and manners, so he knocked on the door. Because of his impatience and confusion, he more hammered on the door than knocked.

'Katrina? Are you awake?' Mick yelled. He heard a muffled groan from the room.

'Well I am now,' said a sleepy and annoyed voice.

'We have men outside who are blocking us in. Did I tell you about the Evil San? Well, his men are just outside.'

A loud thump came from the room.

'Are you alright?' Mick asked through the door.

'Yeah, absolutely fine. I'll just get changed and I'll be right out. You'll want to know where the security stuff is, right? Well, if you turn the clock in the living room, a door will open to the right of the mantelpiece. You should know what to do from then.'

Mick ran down the stairs and did what she said. The door opened and he ran in. He saw the emergency button and hit it.

Immediately, a door opened into another room. In this room, there were lots of security buttons, surveillance camera screens, and guns (with knock-out darts, of course). There were gun attachments so they could fix them to banisters etc.

Mick ran and sat in the only seat in the room. He turned on all the surveillance cameras. Mick noticed that a lot of focus was being placed on the front of the house, but the back of the house, which lead to the bottom of the road, was not being watched at all. It was easy to get out, and that would be their getaway if it came to it.

Mick then pushed all the 'lock-down' switches down. Metal panels slammed down in front of the windows, and the front door. He left the back door open.

Then he grabbed as many guns and emplacements as possible and ran out of the room. He ran into Katrina on the way out. A few guns fell from his hands.

'Oh, sorry...'

She picked them up. Mick again was stunned. She was wearing a complete covert ops suit, but in female version. She looked good in it. Also, he noticed it was leather, and was body tight. Mick made himself busy with the guns to distract himself from her. They set up the guns and then Mick got into a spare covert ops suit (male version obviously) and put his spare ammunition in the spare pockets.

As they were finishing off the final touches, they heard a loudspeaker coming from the outside.

'WE GIVE YOU 5 MINUTES TO GIVE YOURSELVES UP. OTHERWISE WE WILL FORCE YOU OUT. YOU WILL NOT BE ABLE TO RESIST. JUST LOOK OUTSIDE.'

They looked outside through a slight crack in the metal. There, standing as a rabble, were about 40 men, with an extra 10 sorting out the vans. On top of each one was a machine gun. It would be impossible to escape out that way. That is, if they survived the attack that would soon be coming.

Giving themselves in never even popped into either of their minds.

Mick briefly explained his plan to Katrina, to which she agreed, (with a few changes), and then stationed themselves for the fight.

After a few minutes, the loudspeaker came on again.

'YOUR TIME HAS ELAPSED. WE WILL COME IN AND GET YOU. WE WERE GIVEN ORDERS TO TAKE YOU ALIVE IF POSSIBLE, BUT TO US, THAT IS OF NO IMPORTANCE. NOW; ADVANCE!'

The battle of Baker's House had begun.

A few men moved forwards. Mick couldn't see where they went or what they were doing, but Mick could guess.

They were trying to blow up the door.

Mick had to move because otherwise he would be blown apart! He ran up the stairs just in front of him and waited in silence.

A few seconds later...

BOOM!

An almighty crash came from the door as the supports for the door came crashing down. Then there was calm as the dust started to settle.

But not for long however, as machine gun fire came hurtling through the door. The bullets tore open a cupboard that stood just in front of the doorway. It was a slight hindrance, but it was not going to delay them long.

They pushed it out of the way and then started to search for Mick and Katrina in the living room, which was just to the left of the door.

Katrina was sitting there, crying her eyes out.

'I didn't know he was bad!' she was wailing, 'I didn't realize he was in trouble!'

As was expected, the men were astounded at this sight. But what they failed to see was Mick halfway up the stairs with a machine gun, exactly opposite the living room.

The sound echoed through the house long after he had stopped firing.

Mick had fired at a group of men who had gone into the room, but more had come in just at the last second, also getting caught in his fire.

'*Perfect!*' Mick had thought. '*The earlier we take them down, the better.*'

Katrina ran out of the living room and up to Mick.

'You got a round dozen, now GO!'

Mick jumped down the stairs and rolled into the dining room which was right next to the living room. There he picked up two handguns and got into a kneeling position. Both of them held their breath. Mick suddenly heard the sound of feet crunching up the driveway. Then more feet joined it. Eventually, he heard someone enter the house. Mick peeped round the door. There was a man in the doorway, peeping into the living room. Happy there was no one in there, he walked into the house and turned to face the stairs...

PPHHT!

Something flashed through the light and suddenly the man was slumped against the banister, his tongue lolling out and something thin and silver sticking out of his neck.

Mick saw Katrina give him the thumbs up, but he did not return, for something else had taken up his mind.

Five more men were running into the house, and aiming at an unprepared Katrina.

This is what Mick had prepared for however. He got into a crouching position, and then flung himself sideways into the hall. As he did, he aimed as well as he could (it is difficult to aim properly whilst flying about two feet above the ground and moving pretty fast) and fired his guns at the men.

He fell back onto the floor, hard, and looked up, expecting men to be towering over him. But his aiming had been pretty good. He had got the first two men, and they had blocked up the doorway. Katrina had dealt with the other three and the one who lagged on the end.

'Come on, get upstairs!' Mick yelled at Katrina, as he picked himself up off the floor. He ran after her, up the stairs. On the landing, Mick opened one of his pockets and pulled out a stun grenade. He put it on the floor and pulled out another one. Then he picked them up and got them in easy readiness for priming and then throwing.

As expected men came charging in with ferocity, hoping to take them unexpected, but Mick had expected the unexpected. When they realized that they had moved they started searching.

By now, the entrance hall was full of people; the perfect time to throw a grenade.

Mick primed the grenade and threw it. It was an impact grenade, so when it hit someone's head, it blew up. Mick and Katrina threw themselves onto the floor to avoid the shock wave. Once their hearing had come back they risked getting back onto their feet.

They looked over the banister and saw that the floor was littered with unconscious bodies. About five of them were stirring, but Katrina took them out with a few well placed shots from her own Walther P22.

'Time to split up, I guess.' Katrina whispered in Mick's ear.

'Yeah. See you later. Good luck!'

'You to!'

Mick ran off to the ladder in Katrina's parents' room. Up he climbed and arrived in the attic. In the attic was a concealed flap, the sole purpose of which was to give access to getting outside when the house was in lock-down mode.

Mick opened the flap a crack and looked outside. There he could still see a lot of men waiting to attack. They were obviously taking no chances.

Mick checked the distance between himself and the edge of the roof.

'*I think I can reach the men,*' thought Mick.

From behind him, he heard the sudden chatter of a machine gun. He only hoped it was Katrina's.

He looked outside again and looked at the vans. They were out of his reach. The grenade would never hit either van. He really wanted to take those machine guns out.

But the gun would.

Mick reached down and pulled out his Beretta 92FS. Then he reached into a different pocket and pulled out a silencer. He screwed it onto the gun. He aimed carefully. He was not able to destroy the guns, but he might be able to take out the gunners themselves. The problem was they could be replaced. But, at least it would put the guns out of action, even if it was for only a little while.

Mick fired. A very soft *pphhuuuuutt*! came from the gun and a man on the left hand van fell onto the gun with a grunt of surprise.

Again, Mick aimed and fired. The other machine gunner slumped back in his seat, his eyes sliding in and out of focus until they finally closed altogether.

'Mick, could I have some help!' Katrina yelled from downstairs, 'They are hiding from me where I can't see them without being in risk!'

Mick got his last grenade in his hand and stuck his head out of the flap completely. Suddenly, a line from one of those very old American films came to him.

'Hey, you guys! Share this pineapple between you!'

He primed the grenade and chucked at the area near the door. A group of men had come out of the house to see where all the shouting was coming from. Mick assumed that they had not received the full impact of the blast, for he had to duck down quick as a volley of bullets came spraying their way towards him.

As the flap came down behind him, he heard the bullets slam into the tiles beside it, as well as into it. Mick climbed down the ladder and jumped the last few steps. Mick ran over to where he last saw Katrina. He had to go past the stairs to get there. As he reached the top of the stairs, a bullet smashed into the wall beside him. He ducked just as a stream of bullets came ripping out of the shadow from the kitchen doorway. Mick crawled his way along to Katrina, who he now saw huddled against the far wall, cradling the machine gun in her arms.

'I took out some support, but there is a good twenty of them left, not to mention the leaders.' Mick whispered.

'About five of them are in the kitchen.' Katrina answered. 'There is no way of being able to get them without being shot ourselves, so there is no way of getting downstairs. What are we going to do?'

'Did MI5 give you an emergency escape?'

Katrina sat and thought for a moment.

'They might have done...? I know they were planning to, but they might not have finished it.'

'It's our best shot.' Katrina sprang up and ran into her room. Mick followed her.

Inside, Katrina was typing a code into a pad. Seconds later, a section of wall slid back to reveal a hole in the wall big enough to fit a fully-grown man inside. Katrina crawled into it. When she was gone, Mick followed her.

Inside was a small tunnel. It ended with a dead end, but a pole protruding from the ceiling lead into another tunnel going down. Mick grabbed the pole and slid down it.

At the bottom, he found himself in Katrina's base. She herself was already getting ready to open the door.

'Try to be as quiet as possible.' Then he added as an afterthought, 'Does that door make a noise when...'

CLANG! The door gave out a loud hiss and went straight into the ceiling.

'...it opens?'

Mick grabbed Katrina's machine gun from her hands and trained it onto the door in the living room. As he suspected, 5 men came running in. He fired a volley at them, make them fall unconscious.

'Come on!' Katrina was yelling at him. Whilst he was firing at the men, she had broken through the glass door and was ready to escape.

'Not yet. I have an idea.' Mick threw the machine gun to Katrina, then grabbed two sub-machine guns, and walked to the door.

Mick waited until he could hear someone. He heard a crack as someone stepped onto some wood and broke it. Mick ran quickly across the hall to cover, firing both guns at the men there. They had no time to react. Mick slipped on a piece of wood and fell to the floor. When Mick got up, he found men piled up in the hall. Half the doorway was blocked with the amount of bodies piled up.

'Well, we've had a blast!' Mick said to the unconscious men.

Mick ran out to Katrina who was waiting outside. She gave him a puzzled look, but all he would say is, 'We're safe for now.'

They climbed over the fence at the back of the garden and walked round the block to the street.

When they got there, they discovered 5 men waiting to go into the house.

'I'll take them.' Mick said, but Katrina stopped him.

'No, I will. I need to have some fun as well, you know!'

Katrina got up and crept round the corner. Stealthily, she made her way round the back of them. She got to the one at the back, and tapped him on the shoulder. When he turned around, she said,

'You are under arrest for breaking and entering, for vandalism and stealing.' The man pulled his gun out but Katrina grabbed his arm, rolled over his back and pointed the gun in her enemy's hand at the others. She pushed a nerve, which made his index finger twitch. The gun went off. The other 4 men fell to this gun, and then she pointed it at the man himself and made him fire it at himself.

Mick came round and clapped her on the back.

'Impressive! Well done. Now we've both had our fun, we need to tidy up this mess.'

Just as he said that, the back doors of the vans opened, and three men got out.

They were dressed like ninjas.

'Hey, fancy dress party?!' Mick jested.

That was a big mistake, for suddenly one of them made a sudden movement with his hand. Something flashed in the air and Mick felt something cut across his face. In the wall behind them was stuck a small silvery disk, with jagged and pointed edges.

'A shuriken.' Katrina muttered. 'What does that mean?'

'It means we run!'

Mick and Katrina ran inside the house and out of sight. Mick felt his cut. It was quite deep and blood was coming out quickly. He grabbed a plaster from one of his pockets and stuck it on.

'That's better. Mick said. 'Now, what do you think we should do? Do you have a sword in your base?'

'A sword?' Queried Katrina. 'Why do we need swords when we have these?' She pointed to the gun she had taken off the man.

'Because...' Mick started to say, but Katrina was already heading towards the front door. Mick watched what happened next with apprehension.

Katrina got her gun and fired five shots at one of the funnily-dressed men. Somehow, with amazing speed and agility, he had two swords in his hands and he had jumped into the air, missing two darts, and deflected the other three with the swords.

Katrina stood stock still, amazed. Mick had to pull her out of harm's way as more shurikens came flying at her, all deadly accurate.

'You're right.' Katrina admitted. 'We need swords. I have some, but how can you beat them. They are so fast. What are we going to do?'

'Oh, well, let us just say I have a little gadget up my sleeve!'

Mick didn't say what it was, but he gave her a flash of a smile, and then ran off to the secret base to look for the swords. Katrina ran over to help; she got the swords out for him to look at and took one for herself. Mick grabbed the two swords he liked; they were just like the ninjas'; long, quite thin, but strong. Mick swung them about to get the feel of them.

'These will do nicely. Right, now, let's get out there!'

Mick ran out of the room and out of the house. When Katrina got out there, she found Mick standing facing them. When they saw her, they started to throw shurikens at her. She ran back into the house; all the shurikens thudded into the wall. So Mick was all alone to face the three ninjas.

Before Katrina had reached Mick, the ninjas had already tried throwing the shurikens at him but he had blocked or dodged them all with such skill as can't be imagined. So the ninjas came up with a new plan; take him out with pure force. But Katrina had butted in at that moment, so they aimed at her instead. Once she was out of the way, the ninjas came at him again.

Now, if someone was attacking you, you would normal assume that they would charge at you or circle you. But it was not so with the ninjas. They split apart into different directions; one going right, one going left, and the other going straight at him. Even when they came at him, it was in such a peculiar manner that Mick was thrown for a moment as what to do. They were cart-wheeling, jumping and rolling to get at him.

Mick regained his composure in time to parry the first man, who came over from a one-handed cart-wheel, slashing down at him with both swords and the second man with the other who had come in low at his feet. Then they both sprang away. The third man had got behind Mick, so he threw himself backwards onto the ground, bringing both swords up to catch the enemy sword, which was swung at him with both hands, between them.

Mick now noticed that this manoeuvre had left him venerable. He was flat on the ground with his swords above his head, his whole body unprotected. So Mick acted on impulse.

The adrenalin rush that always occurs in these sorts of situations let Mick do something so amazing he himself wouldn't have believed he had done it, if Katrina had not told him she had seen it herself.

Mick slid his swords upwards and, with the swords lax in his hands, grabbed the wrists of the ninja. Mick then pulled himself up, lashing out with his foot at an approaching ninja. It caught him right in the face. Mick continued to pull himself upwards and eventually pulled himself over the head of the ninja, his arms pulled over him. He let go of the man's wrists and grabbed the sword instead, yanking it out of the man's grip. Then he dropped all three swords and grabbed the ninja's clothes at the shoulder. He then threw himself on the ground and, with all his strength, threw the ninja over the top. The man flew into a wall and crumpled in a heap. Mick did a back roll, got himself up and picked up the swords. He slid the ninja's sword into one of his sheaths and picked up his own and got himself into the ready position; ready to fight!

Since there were only two of them left, he could fight easier. His only problem was that one of them had two swords. To match the three swords of the ninjas Mick could not do. After all, he only had two hands! But he could gain another.

'Katrina, could I have a hand?' Mick yelled.

'But I'll get killed if I come out! I'm not good enough to fight them!' She yelled back.

'No, I mean literally!'

'What?' She was puzzled for a moment until she realised what he was talking about. 'Oh!' She ran back inside. When she came back she was carrying in her hands a fake arm.

'I've got it!' She yelled back to him. Now she saw him fighting the two men off. He was doing badly, since he was one sword down. When he saw her, he ran towards her. She held the arm out, and as he ran past he grabbed it. Katrina hurried back inside so the ninjas couldn't harm her. Of course, one of them could have gone and taken her out, but they knew they needed strength in numbers to take down Mick. Both of them could take him out.

Or so they thought. For Mick had now got an extra arm. It was an arm that was mechanical and had some wires leading out of it. It also had a harness for attaching it to himself. Mick slung it on. Then he found the 'on' switch and pressed it. Suddenly, the bare wires which were touching his skin came alive and pushed themselves into the skin. Mick shuddered. Then he stopped and moved his extra arm.

It worked! The arm moved as if he had had it all his life. He grabbed the other sword at his hip and put it up into the proper position.

The ninjas who had been advancing upon him slowly now saw what had happened. Although he couldn't see their faces, he could sense their shock and amazement.

'I'm a three-armed fighting machine,' Mick yelled, 'and you don't want to mess with me!'

Then he charged again. This time, they were even; three swords versus three swords.

As Katrina watched from the door way, she marvelled at them. Not just Mick but all of them. The way they fought was amazing. They were a blur of motion, each intermingling with the other. There were the two ninjas with their amazing acrobatics, each using the other to try and best Mick.

But they couldn't, for Mick was weaving in and out, blocking all the attacks and putting in some attacks of his own.

Suddenly, Katrina had a sudden longing to fight. She could feel a power rising up inside her and knew she could do it. She picked up her own sword and ran up as silently as she could behind the ninjas. When she was about ten feet behind them she threw herself onto the ground. Nobody had seen her. She noticed that the ninjas were being pushed back. One of them came within a hands breadth of stepping on her. Katrina spun herself around and drove her knee hard into the back of the ninja's knee. He collapsed, and Katrina smacked him on the head with the flat of her sword. He fell, dazed. She got up and swung her sword at the last remaining ninja. He blocked it and started to attack her. She returned the favour and blocked them in return. She surprised herself at how fast she was moving, as she retreated under the onslaught but it lessened as Mick joined the fray. Now it was the ninja who was outnumbered 4 to 1. His end came quickly as from nowhere there came the sound of sirens; the police had come. The ninja, knowing he was beaten, tried to run for it, but he ran straight into Katrina, who gave him a punch right in the face, knocking him out cold.

'We did it!' Katrina yelled.

'Yes, we sure did.' Mick muttered to himself with a grin on his face.

Then the police came with John and some MI5 clean-up men.

The aftermath of the battle was not very exciting in the end. All the bodies were cleared away, and Mick and Katrina had to give an account of the battle. Mick was then told he could go home, for that had been sorted out.

When he got home, he found a letter that had been left. It said that both his and Katrina's parents had been sent off to a facility to keep them out of the way. He also found out that his and Katrina's siblings were being sent there to help them forget about the ordeal.

When Mick went upstairs to bed (the cleanup had taken most of the day) he found that the boss wanted to speak to him.

Mick went into his secret base and turned on the P.C.

'Well, Mick, it looks like you have had an eventful day.'

'Yes, Katrina too.'

'Oh, yes, of course. Well now to business.' Mick suppressed a smirk. 'Since the Evil San knows where you live, it would be best if you move.'

'No way, hosé. I ain't moving anywhere.'

'Ok, well, I think we need to move our plan forward. Tomorrow, I want you to go into that garage, take a look around and take any pictures you can, but do not take any undue risks. We don't want you killed.

'Alright boss. But it will have to be in two days. My organizer needs to be fixed.'

'Well, two days then, but as soon as you can; I expect it.' With that, he signed off.

'Aiy, aiy, aiy. This is going to be a heck of a time.'

The Enemy Base

Three days later, as it came to be, Mick found himself standing outside the school with Katrina and John. It was lunch-time, so they had to be careful. They didn't want to be spotted by a teacher.

'Right,' Mick said, 'I'm going in first. You two watch the building and you are to be on constant alert. If I need to contact you, it will be by the organizer. Take your bikes with you. We may need a quick getaway.

'Now, if I am any longer than half an hour, one of you come and find me. If it doesn't feel right, then just get away and tell the boss. You understand?'

'Sure,' they both answered.

'Well, then; see you later. I hope.' And with that, he picked up the bag with his gadgets in and ran around the corner and onto the street.

'So,' Katrina started after a while, 'when do we head off?'

'In a couple of minutes. We need to give him time to get there. If someone saw all three of us coming round the corner, they would easily catch on.' John stifled a yawn. 'No matter how dumb they are.

'You used to this role then?' Katrina asked.

'I'm bored stiff with it. Sometimes I feel I could achieve more, but I don't know. I've never been given the chance. Neither has Mick for that; this is his first time. But I have always been the second in command behind him.'

'Why don't you move to another district? Then you could be the top kid. And you wouldn't have to compete with Mick, either.' John stayed silent. 'So? Why don't you?'

'I don't know. There's something...' He faded off. He thought for a moment and then said,

'You know people say that twins, especially identical ones, have a bond between them. If one is hurt, the other will sense it, stuff like that.'

'Yes, I have heard that. And that the bond will grow, even if they don't know each other.'

'Exactly! It is something like that. But I don't see how we could be twins. I guess that it must be our friendship that has grown after the years. Well, only time will tell, eh? Time for me to go.'

So off he went to get into his position. Katrina had noticed the sudden change of subject, and thought she had just hit upon a soft spot.

* * *

Whilst John and Katrina had been talking, Mick had made his way over the road. The place was empty because of the lunch break. There were two entrances into the garage; one for cars and one for the staff. Mick was opposite the staff entrance. He decided to go in there first. He would probably get more answers there.

He crept up to the entrance and slipped inside. There were two doors on the left-hand wall. The room he was in now was more or less empty except for a few petrol tanks near the back. In each of the doors were a little window and notice. The left door was labelled 'office' and the right 'staff'. He headed towards the staff door and peeped inside. There were three men sat down drinking coffee, all facing a plasma TV that was against the opposite wall.

Suddenly, one of them got up. Mick ducked back down. He could hear a voice with a strong cockney accent coming closer.

'...and da boss wants anover free cars by tommora, aw righ'? I gotta go an' keep watch now. See ya later.'

He crept along to where the petrol cans were and slid in behind them. The door opened and one the men came out. He pulled the door to and then walked out of the garage and around the corner. He seemed to have popped to the corner shop just down the road.

Mick listened to check if anyone else was coming, then he snuck out and into the room labelled 'office'. He closed the door quickly behind him. Inside this room there was a desk, a chair, some drawers, and nothing else. He put down his bag of gadgets on the desk and looked around. He opened the drawers and found them empty. It was obviously new. The whole room looked new, for that matter. The desk had nothing on it, and the walls were bare.

Mick put on his 3-D goggle game and turned the backlight on and off three times and selected the x-ray mode. The display suddenly turned black and white. The walls in the room were black with the objects in the room white. But at the back of the room there was a grey and fuzzy rectangular object, about three metres up and one across. Mick walked closer to it. It looked like a lift (and Mick did not stop to presume that it was not) but how to get to it was the problem.

He turned off the goggles and slung them around his neck. He felt over the wall to see if he could find some kind of opening or switch that would allow him access to the lift. There were no cracks at all in the wall. There was nothing to show that a lift even existed. Then he remembered the words of a very wise dwarf from a movie he had recently watched about certain doors that were not meant to be seen or found.

After a few minutes of searching the desk for a switch, he gave up. There was nothing to find there. He put the goggles back in the bag and walked out of the office. He looked out to see if the watchman had got back yet. He hadn't. Mick crept along the wall to the other entrance; the cars' entrance.

He took a peep around the corner, and when he was sure no one was there, he went in. This room was the work area. The garage was so small that it could only work on one car at a time. The rest waited outside.

There was no car in the garage at that moment, which meant that the ramp which pushed the car up was left exposed. Since it was, Mick noticed something. On the floor around it was a circle. Not a drawn circle, but a crack in the floor, which ran round the whole thing. Mick thought he had found the reason for the disappearing cars.

He stood in the centre of the circle and got out his goggles again. He turned them on, and put them into the electricity-detecting mode. Everything went dark, except for a small line of white on the floor. The white was electricity, so Mick assumed that it was a wire. It ran to the jack in the ramp. With his foot, he pressed the jack down. Suddenly everything turned a bright white before his eyes. He tore the goggles from his head. The whole floor was moving upwards. No, the circle of floor he was standing on was moving down! The flash of light had been the electricity to take it down.

He waited for it to reach the bottom. When it did, he found himself in an underground cross-road. Six tunnels led off of it. Each of them had a label above it. They read; 'Boss' quarters', 'lift', 'exit', 'mess room', 'sleeping quarters' and 'workroom/storage'.

'*The Evil San sure does like to be organized,*' Mick thought to himself.

He got out his personal organizer and sent off a message to John and Katrina to tell them how to get down into what seemed to be the head of operations. Once it was sent, he headed down the tunnel labelled 'workroom/storage'.

As he went down the tunnel, smaller tunnels led off of the larger one. Mick could only guess where they went.

Finally, he reached the end of the tunnel. At the end was a vast room that was stuffed full with cars. Cars were piled on top of each other, with only small gaps between them for walking through. Mick worked his way into the room. As he moved further in, he saw that some of the cars had bits pulled off of them. Sometimes the whole body had been ripped off, leaving the chassis exposed, the parts clinging to each other feebly.

Mick continued through the room, and as he reached the back he saw two doors. He headed towards them. He was closer to the left hand door, so he took that one first.

Mick gasped. There, right in front of his eyes, was what looked like a massive engine. There were boilers, petrol tanks, pipes, and wires all over the place. Large pipes led off of it and into the rock.

As Mick took his eyes off the machine, he noticed some work stations behind it. He walked over to them. Some equipment lay on them, and it looked like the engine still wasn't finished. He looked closer at the equipment and noticed that it was the same equipment he had seen in Gareth Hunsan's secret room.

He found some of the bigger pieces and was able to match them to others he could see on the engine. Again, like in Gareth's room, he found the technology different from normal, but still familiar. It looked new. Where would they find any new...

Then it hit him. And it hit him hard. He ran out of the room and took the other door. In that room was a pile full of the technology.

He ran as hard as he could and headed for the crossroad. How could he be so forgetful? He had seen that technology in the CCTV footage that his boss had show him of the new prisons! Now he had an idea that whatever the Evil San was doing, it was going to be big, and definitely disastrous.

He had reached the cross-roads. He was about to head up the 'exit' tunnel, when the sign 'boss' office' caught his eye. If the Evil San was Gareth, it couldn't hurt to take a quick peep.

He set off. He started to think whether the Evil San could be Gareth, but he didn't think it likely. Gareth had been rather unintelligent at his school. He would never have been able to pull anything as big as this off. He shunted aside the idea that he could have had some hired help, because it made his stomach churn.

He eventually made it to the door at the end of the tunnel. He tried the door, but as he suspected, it was locked. Luckily, thanks to Johnny Johnson, he had a lock pick hidden in his P.O. He picked the lock with ease, which made him start to think that things were becoming a little too easy for his liking. He crept into the room and closed the door. It was pitch black in the room. He sat down against the door and felt along the wall for the light switch. He found it and flicked it on.

Light flickered on. It had come on immediately, but a silenced machine gun had started firing also. It stopped after about a minute.

Mick got up off the floor. Since he had been sat down, the bullets had gone straight over his head.

'Phew, that was a close shave,' he said.

He got up and walked over to the desk. He sat down. As he did, his foot caught a trip wire, and right past his neck, where the heart would usually be on an adult, a dagger flew past. It just clipped him, sending a pearl of blood down his neck.

He ignored the pain and searched the drawers, being very careful in case they were booby-trapped. He found the blueprints to a machine like nothing he had seen before. From the appearance, it was massive. It would also explain the massive engine. Obviously, the bodies of the cars would make the body of the machine, but how long it would take to make and how it would get into the open, he had no idea. Nor did he know where it was being built.

He stood up ready to leave, but as he did, his knees hit the bottom of the desk. Something turned over, and Mick guessed that there must be a hidden drawer there. He got down on his hands and knees and looked at the underside of the desk. There, strapped to a hidden turn-over drawer, was a piece of elemancilin that was easily recognizable.

It was an electricity immobilizer with an electricity container attached. It was an important piece of equipment in the prisons because it would stop all electrical devices from working by literally sucking the electricity out of it.

Suddenly, Mick could see exactly what the Evil San was doing.

'And you're not going to get away with it!' Mick said to himself.

But he heard the sound of guns being cocked. He got up from under the desk and looked up. Five men with machine guns trained on him stood around the room.

He could see the silhouette of someone framed in the doorway, clapping.

'Well done, Mick, well done indeed. But I thought that even you would have expected a fingerprint recognition device on the door handle! Oh, and by the way, I think you will find I *am* going to get away with it!'

Mick froze. His worst fears had just come true. It was Gareth Hunsan.

The Evil San

'Mick, I continue to be surprised at your lack of caution.'

It was ten minutes later and Mick was in a cell, bound with rope to a chair. There were two men on the door and two in the room, along with Gareth Hunsan.

'Well anyway,' Gareth was saying, 'It is to the basic interrogation that I hope you're familiar with Mick. So; who sent you, who is with you, and more importantly, what do you know?'

'Answer it yourself, Gareth.' Mick put all the malice he could into that short sentence. One of the guards gave him a back-handed slap right across the face. His eyes flashed and he tasted blood in his mouth. He must have bitten his tongue.

'You call the Evil San by his proper name. You do not call him with that junk of a word.' The guard told him. He was a strong, black man, but was not any ordinary guard. He had many medals on his uniform, and had a sense of authority about him. He was a man to be feared, yet also respected.

'Yes, by the way, do you like the name?' Gareth interrupted.

'Well…' Mick thought for a moment, and then said, 'I guess you took the 'san' from '*Hunsan*'. Not very original. Though I guess you were the class dump at school.'

Mick closed his eyes and braced himself for another slap, but none came. He opened his eyes and looked up to find Gareth holding the general's arm back, which was raised to hit Mick again. Gareth was doing so with surprising ease, since the strong man seemed intent on hitting Mick. Mick now thought that he might have misjudged Gareth slightly.

'Don't worry, Tomodan. He just needs to learn some respect. Something Mick obviously hasn't learnt. Control yourself; we'll get him later. Wait a minute...' He looked at Mick with surprise and puzzlement. 'Why don't **you** have a code name - a secret identity? Have you never bothered to ask for one?'

'No.' Mick kept it clean this time.

Gareth laughed.

'Mick you are so very dull. You never had any fun. Well, not proper fun. Always the book worm, always the student. You never livened up, had some fun.'

'Well, in fact, I did.' Mick retorted. 'But only when you turned your back. How could anyone have fun looking at that hideous face of yours.'

This time it was Gareth's turn to hit him. This time it really hurt.

'Well, Mick, I'll give you a code name. You can be called... the Unknown Kid. Because you will be the kid spy that will never be known! You will die here, without ever seeing sunlight again. Since it is so, I'll explain my life to you, from where you left it. And it was thanks to you, and John for that matter, that it happened this way. How fitting.

'The last time you saw me was at my 11th birthday party. You had given me an electrical watch that had a tin opener, a lock pick, along with many other things. John had given me a 'make-your-own-goo' set. I put on your watch, and then started to play with the goo set. Unfortunately, I spilled some goo onto the watch. I went through some of the functions that the watch did to see if it still worked. I got to the mini chainsaw and then it stopped. Thinking it had broken, I put it on the table outside beside the pool and then I went into the pool for a swim. Suddenly the watch started to work again, and the motor was going so fast it fell off the table and into the water.

Now let me explain what happened next. The goo had reacted with the metallic plastic of the watch, burnt a hole in it and had then burnt into the wires. Some of them were also fried. Then, when it fell in the water, I got electrocuted. Luckily for me, I was only just getting in after having a break. I had just dunked my head in when it happened. Somehow, I survived, but after that, I hated electricity. So I have decided to rid the world of it one country at a time. First the United Kingdom, then the rest of Europe, and so on and so forth. I will have the elemancilin and the novenicity, the perfect electricity, taking me to into 22nd century, whilst the rest of the world will be plunged back into the Dark Ages! I will be the ruler of the world, and no one will be able stop me!'

Gareth had started to become quite mad the further he continued in his story.

'*That electric shock must have addled his brain,*' Mick thought, as Gareth started a high, demented laugh.

'You're deranged!' Mick yelled.

Gareth stopped laughing and looked at him. 'Do you know, Unknown Kid, you are quite right. I am deranged, and anyone would be after what happened to me.'

It was Mick's turn to laugh this time.

'Do you mean to say that you are the best outcome of the situation you were in?'

'Yes.'

'Well, then you are mental!'

'SHUT IT!' Gareth had gone wild. He kicked the legs of the chair that Mick was sitting on which shattered into splinters. He picked Mick of the floor and pinned him against the wall.

'Do you know where my name, "The Evil San" has also come from?' He spoke in barely a whisper, but Mick could hear every word as clearly as if he were shouting them.

'I got it because I have become a master of martial arts. I know every single one and can use any one of them at need. In fact, I was taught by the grandest of masters, Himo D.I. Karagammaro, whose plan to knock down Big Ben you foiled about a month ago. It was also he who set me up here and taught me how to run it.

You said I was unintelligent earlier. Well, you were wrong. At school, I found everything so boring, so unimportant. But when I knew what my calling was, my purpose, I threw myself whole heartedly into the learning process. I became very knowledgeable in how to run this place and how to work with the other people. That is the most important skill I have learnt. It has put me among the best. The mafia's cannot touch me because they cannot work together. Me and my Master have higher aims than the common rebel, thug, or crime leader.

My Master bestowed upon me this name in respect for what I had achieved. The Japanese, of which he is one, call anyone 'san'. Have you not heard it said, 'Mick-san'? I'm sure you have. The "Evil" is self-explanatory. Understand?'

'NOW ANSWER MY INITIAL QUESTIONS!!!'

He had roared the last sentence in Mick's ear and dropped him on the floor. Mick sat on the floor, dazed. Once he had come round to his senses, he decided to cooperate with them more.

At least a little bit more anyway.

'Alright. Well I know you know the answer to the first question; MI5. I suspect you also know the answer to the second question also. John Corton is backing me up. And the third, you told me nearly all of it yourself.

'I know practically everything. I know that my hunches are correct after what you just told me. You are going to use the cars to make the body of the electricity-stealing machine and their engines as the engine. I have already seen it. It is a marvellous piece of machinery. Pity it is being used for the wrong purposes. By the way, where are you building it?'

'I am tired, Unknown Kid, of your tiring and frankly rubbish, petty jokes. But as to your question, do you really think I would answer it if you were not already in it.' Gareth got up off the chair he had sat back on and walked towards the door. 'I'll be back to teach you some manners though. Tomodan, you can give him half an hour to think things through. Then you can have your turn.'

Mick was stunned at The Evil San's answer. The whole complex of tunnels was the machine!

The Evil San walked out, with Tomodan and the guards following. Only one guard was left to guard him. This guard then shut the door and locked it.

The door had a lock with a padlock over the top of it. There was no way out.

The cell had no windows and was solid concrete. His hands were still tied together, but his legs had come undone when Gareth had smashed the chair. He sank down to his knees and then lay down.

After about twenty minutes, Mick heard a noise coming from down the end of the corridor. Round the corner peeped a head that Mick recognized all too well.

Mick remembered that he still had his shark tooth necklace on that doubled as a stun dart. He tried to pick it up with his bound hands. He eventually did, but when he looked up, the guard was lying unconscious at the feet of John.

'I could have made it easier, you know.' Mick said.

'Yeah, but I could not just let you get all the fun could I?' John said with a smirk.

'How did you know I was in here?'

'I heard this guy bragging about how he would beat you up before the Evil San could.' John paused. 'I think I saw the Evil San. And if I did, I don't like it. How could Gareth do such a thing?'

'I really don't know, but I think his brain is addled. Come on, get me out of here.'

'Stand back,' John cautioned.

John got out his necklace and put the six beads that hung round the tooth in his lips. He squeezed it three times and the tooth shot out at the locks. There was a small explosion and smoke blossomed from the lock. When it cleared, a hole stood where the lock used to be.

John then used the laser on his P.O. to free Mick's hands.

'Come on let's go!'

'Wait a minute, I can't go without my gadgets.' He picked up his bag of gadgets from the chair where they had dumped them.

'Right, now let's get of here.'

They headed down the corridor to the tunnel. Mick followed John since he had lost his bearings of the place. The crossroads were in sight when suddenly a klaxon went off.

PRISONER ESCAPED! HIGH PRIORITY! WARNING!

Tomodan's voice sounded over the klaxon.

'Great!' Mick thought. *'He must have come early to beat it out of me, and found me recently gone.'*

They got to the crossroads and saw men coming towards them from every direction. All but one. No one was coming down the exit tunnel.

'Well, duh!' He thought to himself.

'Don't worry, John, we'll be out of this in a jiffy.' John had pulled out his guns and was firing them at those people who were gaining fastest. But there were too many for him to hold off.

'What are you doing!' He cried.

'Looking for this!' Mick had been digging in his bag. When he came out, he was holding the torch.

'We're meant to be getting out of here! Blinding them won't do much good!'

'It will if I blind them all!'

'But how are you going to do that!'

'Put your oxygen mask on! Now, for a bit of magic; the disappearing act!'

Putting on his own oxygen mask, Mick pulled out the battery, pressed the '+' sign three times and threw it hard on the ground. It detonated on impact.

A billowing cloud of pure white smoke poured from the smashed battery. Soon, the whole of the crossroad was full of smoke. Mick grabbed John's arm and ran for the 'exit' tunnel. Mick had been facing it when the smoke bomb had gone off. They made it through and burst straight out of the smoke. They were near the end of the tunnel, and they could see a lift at the other end. They got in it and pressed the 'up' button.

'Warn me next time before you pull a stunt like that!' John was slumped against the back wall. He had had no idea what Mick was going to do.

'I thought you had the gadget yourself?'

'I forgot about it, all right?'

Mick started to laugh.

'What's so funny?'

'One of the best spies in England, and he loses his cool in a battle where there are no guns aimed at him and he has another teenage spy next to him!'

'I didn't..!' John looked exasperated. 'What do you…?'

'All right, drop it. Contact Katrina and tell her to take "Experiment X" and have some ready for us. We are going to need more speed than a bike will give us.

"Experiment X" was an instant muscle booster. It only worked in the legs, for some unknown reason. But when it was used, they could make you run at speeds of up to 80mph, without getting tired, for around an hour. Unfortunately the only mode of transport it worked on were a pair of specially adapted roller skates. Luckily, that was John's favourite mode of transport. It was not Mick's. He preferred his bike, but the bikes would always break. However though he didn't like roller skates, he could still use them fairly well.

The lift stopped. They both got out their guns and pointed them out as the lift doors opened. There was no one there.

They had arrived at what looked like a back yard. There were tons of tyres, junk and rusty old cars there, along with some petrol cans, one of which was leaking. There was a gate in front of them which was at the side of the garage. Katrina was stood over the road. When she saw them, she ran over to them and jumped over the gate. It took her about a second or two. She actually overshot, careering into Mick and knocking him flat. She found herself lying on top of Mick.

'Oh sorry...'

She blushed so much she looked like she had got bad sunburn.

She got up and got her own bag. From that she pulled out two pairs of roller skates and two needles. She gave one of each to both of the boys. They put the needles in their legs and put half of the drug in each. Then they slid the roller skates on and strapped them up tight. When they were ready they slowly went out of the gate and onto the road. Whilst their backs had been turned the guard had come out the guard room and had spotted them. He stood there gawping at them until they spotted him. Shocked that he had been seen, he had fumbled at his neck for an emergency warning. John brought his gun up and shot him, but it was too late. The man had pressed the button.

'Good luck. When you get home, contact boss and tell him to wait. I have urgent news for him.' A few guards had come out of the guard room.

Another load of men had started pouring out of the back entrance. The people they had met at the crossroads had obviously guessed which way they had gone after overcoming the sedative.

'Let's go!' John called.

'Hang on!' Katrina said quickly. She pulled out a flare from her bag and pointed it at the oncoming men. She pulled the trigger and a red flame shot out of the short butt. It flew towards the men and went past them as they scattered. Instead, the flame hit the petrol that had leaked from its can. The petrol caught light and the rest followed suit. It reached the can and then...

BOOM!

The can exploded and set the whole lot of cans off. The men went flying, a good number of them dead.

They quickly decided to get out of there. Mick and John went one way down the road, and Katrina went the other. At the end of the road, Mick turned to see whether Katrina had got away. He was slightly horrified about what she had just done. She was nowhere in sight. But he could see the guards talking into microphones. Then, out of the blue came ten motorbikes. Two headed after Katrina; the rest turned towards Mick. John had gone round the roundabout just ahead and had reached Mick again.

'Come on! Move it!'

Mick did so. He turned round and headed for home. It was now 2:00 and everyone was back at work. Not many cars were on the road. But as they reached the J11 it got a bit busier. They had to slow down as they weaved in and out of the traffic. It was then that the motorbikes caught up. Each one had two people on. One to drive; one to fire a machine gun. They had excellent aim. They got very close to hitting them. Wing mirrors and windows smashed and cracked right beside them as they manoeuvred their way through the traffic.

When the traffic thinned a bit, Mick and John took a couple of shots when they were behind the cars and one or two gunners fell from their bikes. When they were in the open they swerved using each other to pull themselves in different directions and make the bullets miss them.

As they reached the Reading Football Stadium, Mick yelled to John, 'Let's split up.' John gave a nod to show he understood, and headed off behind the football stadium whilst Mick headed into the shopping complex, using some building work to catapult himself over the wall that was in the way. The bikers did the same. Mick looked back. He saw five bikes, two of them without gunners.

Mick got out his phone and called John. When he answered Mick said,

'How come you get fewer men on you than me? Why didn't we get 50/50?'

'Hard luck mate. Looks like you're a hit with the men!'

'I am not...' But John had hung up, '...gay.' John had a weird sense of humour.

As he moved in and out of the parked cars, he took shots at one bike that overtook him. The driver fell to a dart under the arm. The machine hurtled out of control, finally ending with a burst tyre, throwing both men into a wall.

Only four left.

Mick made his way out of the car park and travelled round the roads for many a mile. During that chase he lost one whole bike and another gunner. Three bikes, one gunner. Mick thought for a moment, and then felt for the torch in his pocket. He felt it and the other battery that had fallen out.

He pulled the battery out and threw it behind him. It exploded. Mick did a quick turn around into the smoke and then did another one on the other side. When he came out of the smoke, the bikers were in front of him. They had stopped, leaving them as sitting ducks. Mick took them down with ease.

Within a few minutes he was home. He had built up quite a sweat, even with the muscle boosters.

He got in and went to tell the boss his news. He was quite happy with his days work.

* * *

But someone else was not quite so happy.

'WHAT DO YOU MEAN, THEY GOT AWAY!' Gareth was furious at how they had all got away without any harm done to them.

One biker who had got away from John and a gunner who had fallen off his bike when fighting Katrina were all that had returned.

'Well, sir,' the gunner started, 'the girl kind of distracted us, you know. She went up a ramp over a hedge and when we went over she came back onto the road.'

'And you see,' the other man started, 'the two boys split up. You told us that the Unknown Kid was the priority, so only three of us went after the other. He tricked those two by spinning round and round until they crashed into each other. I decided that I should come back and report to you.'

Gareth stopped the men, got up, and walked out of the room, with Tomodan and Dr. Feanam following. They walked out of the room and headed for Gareth's office.

Doctor, how long till Operation Hydra is ready?

'Another two days, I am afraid, sir.'

Well you had better make it another two hours, or it will be your life on the line.'

'Can we make it three hours?'

'Two and a quarter.'

'Two and three quarters?'

'Two and half, no more.'

'O.K.!'

'Good. I expect it to be fully operational.'

'It will be, but there won't be much armour or covering. It will mainly be rock. The outer casing was the last thing to do.'

'It will be good enough. Tomodan, how are the weapon systems going?'

'They are done, sir. Shall I get my men working for Feanam?

'Yes. Things are coming together at last.'

They had arrived at the Evil San's office.

'Now, both of you, I have a little task for you to do.' Gareth pulled out a suitcase from under his desk.

'In this is a shield from electricity. Anything in a radius of... in a radius of... well, the distance that it would take to fire one bullet, then going to where the bullet landed, firing another and then from where that lands. (The Evil San had never been very good at maths, especially when guessing was involved. He was also never too good at explaining things.)

'Do you mean the perimeter of the shield would be double a gun's range away from us?' Dr. Feanam inquired.

'Um, yes. Understand?'

'Yes sir!' Tomodan immediately answered.

'Um, where do we install it?' Dr. Feanam asked.

'In the engine. Don't ask me where! How would I know, that is why I hired you!

'Now go do your jobs.'

As Tomodan was about to leave the room, he stopped him.

'The men in my office, the men who survived. Exterminate them.'

'With pleasure, sir.'

Once they had been gone a few minutes, Gareth got up and paced the room. All that he had planned for years was about to be put into action, and now Mick Denning was about to stop it. Hopefully the shield would stop him interfering, but who knew how advanced MI5's technology had become?

Well, only time would tell, and Mick had only two and a half hours of it left to find a weakness in his pride and joy. If he could.

The Final Showdown

Mick got changed before he went to report. He was sweaty, dirty, full of splinters, and smelled of smoke.

But, once he was ready, he turned on the PC and found himself staring at a screen that was split in three; one part for the boss, one for Katrina, and one for John.

The moment he appeared everyone gave a sigh of relief. For a millisecond, just as Mick had turned the PC on, he had seen a hint of fear in John and Katrina's faces.

The boss however, never showed that emotion. He had seen so many agents come and go he had got used to it; he was frankly impervious to it. The sigh was the closest emotion that Mick had ever seen the boss show to worry.

'Well guys,' Mick started. He had jumped straight in because the other two had burst in saying how worried they had been.

'Sir, I expect you would like to know what I found out.'

'I sure would,' He replied hotly. 'First time in, you nearly get yourself killed. I would like to know very much. Your career in managing big tasks might be over.'

'Liven up, I have some good news for you!'

'Oh yes? And how much bad news do you have?'

'Not much.'

'Well get on with it then'.

So Mick started to narrate his story, right from when he entered the garage up till when he got home.

'Now sir. I am sure you would like to know word-for-word what happened when I was interrogated.'

'Well, Mick, I would, but unfortunately I already know your peanut-sized brain would not be able to remember it all, when he couldn't even remember my only instruction!'

'Actually, this peanut-sized brain used his personal organizer to record it all. I am afraid that there is no picture, but you can hear it well enough.

I wanted to get a picture of the Evil San, but I couldn't without having it taken off of me.'

'I think I could help you out there. I got a picture of him. In it he also has his macho bodyguard and someone else with him. I will send you a copy now.'

Mick looked down at his inbox, but nothing came through.

'Hey, how come I don't get one?'

'It's on your organizer, peanut-brain.'

'Oh, right.'

'Wait a minute!' the boss exclaimed, 'That man on the left is the head of mechanics and science at Oxford University. He went missing over a year ago. He was presumed dead. It was when he was visiting the site of the meteor. The Evil San must have taken him when he stole the elemancilin and the information on how to use novenicity.'

'So the Evil San has been working for quite some time on this project.' Katrina stated.

'Oh yes, boss. I need to tell you the bad news I haven't told you yet. I overheard someone saying that the machine that the San is building will be ready in two days. You had better get someone to…' But he never finished his sentence, for at that moment Mick started to hear a rumbling, and then the floor started to vibrate.

'It must be an earthquake!' Katrina said with awe. In the UK, the earthquakes were hardly ever very big. It was extremely rare to actually feel it, especially in such a wide radius.

Mick started to spin his chair around whilst he waited for it to calm down. After a couple of revolutions, he started to realize what he was seeing. He stopped and looked out of the window. There, coming out of the ground was a chunk of rock, buildings and mechanical stuff.

It was huge. It had twelve massive wheels, four on each side. Turrets and gun towers came out of everywhere. The garage was flipped over into the rock, to the leave the top flat. Next thing, it was metal. The Evil San surely had stolen an awful lot of knowledge as well as technology. He just hoped the knowledge was in other people's heads.

Mick started to feel sick. He thought of all the people around that area that might have been killed by the earthquake. It must have been high on the Richter scale near the centre. He thought of the school. Hopefully they would have already broken up for the end of the day, but he didn't know.

'Oh macaroni cheese!' He exclaimed.

'Mick, I think it was two hours, not two days.' Someone said. Mick did not see who.

'I think your right,' he replied in shocked, 'Boss, get the specs squadron online and tell them to look for my signal. Get the military in pursuit. Katrina can go with them. Katrina, suit up and get down there! John, you get to your submarines, they may be needed. I can tell that Gareth would pull a stunt like a shield.'

'Wow!' Katrina yelled out.

Mick looked out of the window again and could now see what was so 'wow'. The machine was now a thousand feet in the air.

'It just jumped! That is the best way I can explain it.'

'Don't worry about it, just follow it with the military!'

'Ok, ok, I'm going!'

'Good.'

Mick looked back at the screen and only the boss was there. 'Everything is in order. Get ready to meet up the Spec Squadron.'

'I'm on my way, chief!'

Mick let out a yell of delight. He was about to have the best time of his life; it the time to prove why he had been chosen to join the R.A.F.

Mick ran downstairs, into his back garden, and into the shed. It was rather small and was stuffed full of gardening materials; there were trowels, buckets, spades, bush cutters, shearers, lawn mowers et cetera.

In the corner propped up against the wall were a bunch of spades. Mick picked two up and moved them out the way and then pulled on another.

The door slammed shut and the floor went down into...

A secret cave! There, shining and all ready for use, was his plane. It was a Hawkstrike 6000, full of updated weapons, technology and defence systems that had been developed from the elemancilin and novenicity. They would need it as the Evil San would have it as well.

108

He suited up and jumped into the cockpit. He locked down the hatch and his heads-up display came on.

A smooth feminine voice said,

'What would you like sir.'

'Open top hatch and get me online with the Specs please, Millie.'

'Of course, sir.'

Mick did all pre-flight checks, and then started up his engines. They came on with a roar, but then quieted down to a soft purr.

He made sure the top hatch, or in other words, the roof, was open, and then took off.

Any ordinary plane would have to use a runway, but this one could take off vertically. As he got through the roof, or ground as it was about to become, he pressed a button that closed it up. Then as he rose above the apple tree in his garden, he shot off after the machine that was a red blip on his heads-up map.

But that suddenly disappeared as his squadron came online. His squadron was made up of twelve men, not including himself. They weren't really men, though. They aged from 15 to 20. Mick loved to have people who he could talk to, and that was people who were of a similar age, but slightly old than him; he had always been told he was mature for his age.

'Squad, follow the enemy as far as the sea. If it goes beyond there, wait for me with the army. If not, wait outside the electrical barrier.' Mick said. 'Now, sign in!'

'Specs 1, standing by.'

'Specs 2, standing by.'

'Specs 3, standing by.'

This repeated itself until all thirteen of them were present and correct. Mick was informal, but still had to follow regulations. For roll call, everyone had to use their flight name, but otherwise real names were used.

'Get to the target as fast as you can; that means you too, Jetlag.'

Laughter came across the comm. Jet was always nicknamed Jetlag since he always lagged behind the others, his mind always wandering.

Mick connected himself to Katrina and John. They were to organize the operation, each one of them in charge of a different section of the army; Mick, the RAF, Katrina, the army, and if necessary, John with the navy.

It was best to keep in contact. And anyway, they needed to have a plan.

* * *

Katrina got to the coast and found the Evil San's machine in the middle of the English Channel. She went up to the top of the Cliffs of Dover to get the best overview.

She was in a Hummer v.4 with the head of the army division that was under her. He stood up and used his field glasses to look the sea.

'Look at the size of that thing!' He said. 'How did it get here without crushing the land in between?'

'It jumped.' Katrina said simply.

'Jumped? What gibberish!' He handed her the field glasses. 'How could a thing like that jump here?'

Katrina brought the field glasses to her eyes. 'It didn't jump all the way here. It did it in leaps and bounds.' She looked out over the sea. She could see ships in a certain radius all unable to move. It seemed that the thing did have a shield so that electricity would not work inside. But she could see one navy ship moving towards the... what? She couldn't call it a machine; it was more rock.

'*Target*,' she thought, '*we will call it the target.*'

* * *

I am sure you want to know what this "target" looks like. Well, it was a lump of rock in a roughly cuboid shape. It had a completely flat top, but the sides were riddled with loose rocks and gun turrets of all shapes and sizes. There were certain larger turrets that were in fact energy collectors. These antennas were what pulled the electricity into storage. There were two on both the longer sides, and one on each of the smaller. The whole thing sat on twelve enormous wheels, six on each side.

* * *

The ship was heading toward the target when suddenly a lilac dome appeared out of nowhere as the ship touched it. It passed through. Then when the dome hit the engines, the ship died. The current pushed it away from the dome and, as the ship lost contact with the shield, the shield disappeared so it seemed as if it had never been.

'Get that boat to anchor itself and then get me in contact with the commanding officer,' She said to the driver of the Hummer.

'Yes, ma'am,' said the driver, and he went off to do as she had asked.

After a few minutes wait, the guard came back with a mobile phone.

'The captain of the *Undaunted* on the phone for you, ma'am.'

111

'Thank you.' She took the phone from him. 'Hello? This is Katrina Baker, head of army operations and navy until John Corton arrives. I am part of the S.P.F.T. and I am in command here. Now, I want you to send a small boat back out of this shield. Then get it to anchor half in and half out of the shield so that we can see it.'

'If I may ask, miss,' the captain of the ship replied, 'but why must I do this?'

'It is so when the R.A.F. comes along, they don't fly straight into it and then fall into the sea. They know the shield exists, but they don't know how big it is. It might also show us their attack range. Now get to work, captain.'

'Yes, ma'am!'

* * *

'Captain!' A young orderly came up onto the bridge.

'Yes?' John answered.

'We have come upon the enemy. What are your orders?'

'Settle on the sea-bed just outside their shield. Monitor their sensors; we will need to know when they are going to put their operations into progress.'

'Yes, sir! Oh, and one more thing.'

'Yes?'

'Mick Denning has arrived.'

* * *

When Mick arrived, Katrina, John and himself held a council of war via video link. Together they made their plans. So after half an hour, a plan had been set out and was to be put into operation once the rest of the force was ready. They were still missing two from spec. squadron, three more subs, and the shield that was to protect the on land army from losing electricity.

The day had been pushing on to 3 o'clock when Katrina had arrived. It was 5 o'clock when Operation Counter-Hydra commenced.

Just before that, however, as the last of the men trickled in, Mick suddenly thought, '*I should make a speech! It would be a good idea since we have no idea what is going to happen.*'

He turned on the inter-comm. switch and moved his plane so that it was flying in front of his squadron, who were hovering lined up and ready for battle.

'Men,' he started, 'we are facing an unknown enemy here. Yes, it is true, we know who we are facing. But we don't know what we are facing. Yes, we use it for ourselves, but does that prepare us enough to fight against it? We do not know how they will be played against us. You are going to have to use plain skill and wit. This battle we are about to face will be difficult; the world as we know it will change if this battle is lost. I have faith in you, and I hope to see you all at the end of this.'

He turned off the comm. and switched it so it was in contact with Katrina.

'How did that look?' He asked her.

'Actually, it looked pretty lame. I couldn't hear a thing.'

'Oh. You mean I didn't look cool?'

'Nope.'

'Oh. Well I'll just repeat it then.'

And so he did. He turned on a loud speaker and repeated it at just above ground level.

But at the end he added,

'We fight today a different battle than the battle our grandfathers fought. We begin a new state of warfare, and we will fight so as to put our name in the history books. Most of you dream of the day when you can be known for your actions in the protection of this country. If you are a patriot to England, in whose name we fight, I say today you will gain honour in this battle. You will be known as the men who defended this country without knowing the dangers or whether you would survive. You will be known as the men who took this world into a new era, a better era, an era in which we will make our mark on this world, and we will crush the evil in which we find ourselves facing! In this cause, I say we fight! Gentlemen! Ladies! Pick up your weapons, and we shall advance together and as one!

'FOR ENGLAND!'

'FOR ENGLAND!' A whole chorus of voices swelled from the throats of the men in the air, on the ground and under the sea. And with that the subs activated their special technology, as did specs. squadron, and the army powered up the generators of their shields.

'FORWARD!' And the British forces swarmed in the shield from below and above, at the same moment as missiles propelled themselves into the air from the army. They went straight through the shield and into the rock causing some to fall into the water, but none of the defence turrets were hit and little damage was done.

But the enemy returned the volley. They fired at the quickly incoming fighters.

'Split up, men,' Mick said to his colleagues. 'They are coming in hard with flackers.'

He was not wrong. Heading towards the Specs. squadron were half a dozen missiles that had a golden sheen and a pale white smoke came from their ends. As they got closer, the squadron broke up into twos; a leader and his wingman. One missile went after each group.

The missiles were fast and were faster than the planes. But they did not need to be. The missile that was chasing Mick suddenly put on a burst of speed. It shot straight between the two fighters and stopped in mid-flight just in front of them.

'Flip round and avoid that flacker.' Mick said to his wingman.

'Sure.' He replied.

The pilots started to roll up (or down) and to the side. As they reached the missile, it could be seen that its outer casing had two gaps in the side. From out of these spurted bullets thick and fast. But since the planes were now above and below it instead of to the side of it, the bullets missed. Then the sides started to revolve. The bullets started to move round on a course that would intercept them both!

'Go to maximum acceleration now!' Mick yelled into the comm. There was no need for a reply. Both planes shot off in an increase of speed, leaving the missile behind.

Luckily for the pilots, the flackers only had a limited life span. Once their bullets had been expended, they blew up. And as they pulled away, a golden explosion appeared behind them.

Mick checked his stats. They had all survived, luckily.

'Guys, get in as close to the target as possible. It will be harder for them to use their weapons. Get rid of their defence turrets and the electricity-sucking thingy... You know what I mean! Let's get on with it!'

So far nothing much had happened. The land based army had come to a pause, so they were waiting for more ammunition to arrive and were of not much use until it did. The submarines had so far snuck in unnoticed, but were still too far away to cause any effective damage. But the R.A.F. were still strong and could easily become a nuisance to the enemy. But the Evil San had a plan that would allow him to kill two birds with one stone. It would also give him time to power up his main generators and get his collector online and ready.

Mick looked at his heads up display and saw lots of red blobs coming towards the squadron as it headed towards the target, but there was nothing in front of him. He zoomed in and looked at the altitude of these blobs. They were about 500 feet above him. He looked up.

And he froze. Plummeting towards them, accurately aimed, were huge flaming missiles. They could be angled slightly due to flaps and drag fins that could be controlled by remote.

He came back to his senses and said,

'Everybody look sharp! Flaming missiles coming in 12-2. Nobody do anything until they are within 100 feet. Then move. If you don't then... well, I don't need to tell you. Just get ready.'

Everyone was tense. The missiles fell.

300 feet … 200 feet … 150 feet … 100 feet!

'GO! GO! GO!'

Everyone fled, going in different directions. Up, down, left, right. The missiles changed their course as much as possible, but many of them missed and plunged into the sea. Some of them didn't even come close to hitting the planes. But, as Mick looked down, he saw they had different purposes. Once the steam had cleared, you could see that the area was covered in bubbles. Mick knew what that was. It was the water-enabled bullets that were being fired from the submarines. They were trying to blow them up before they hit the submarines. Mick looked at his screen and winced. One of the submarine lights flickered out, and there were only 11 people left in his squadron.

His throat went tight. But he still managed to say,

'Who's gone?'

'Jet and Phill.' No emotion was in the voice. Either the person who replied was used to it, or he was covering it up extremely well.

'OK.'

'*Just get on with the job*,' he told himself. And he had to as a few more missiles came out of the sky. But by that time, they had reached the enemy and were ready to start taking it apart. Both sides opened fire. Bullets, missiles and lasers flew everywhere. Splashes of light appeared where bullets were absorbed by shields. There were explosions as defence turrets came down. One or two collector turrets fell, but it was too late. When they had arrived, they had started to emit a faint light, but now they were white and glowing. With a sudden force, beams of light shot out then disappeared. Then coming like it usually did, lightning came from all directions flooding into the turrets.

The target was too dangerous to stay close by, because it was impossible to dodge enemy fire and electricity streaming in at the same time. Mick ordered a retreat. When he came out he surveyed the casualties. There were only seven of them left, but one had made it out with a failed engine.

He got all his men to go high over the battlefield, survey, and to help him evaluate what was happening.

'*How are we going to get close now?*' He thought. '*It must have some kind of weakness. What is electricity weak against?*'

He put it out as a general question and got back the answer they needed.

'Well, it's affected by water,' Bob said, 'and we have got plenty of that around.'

'Yes we have!' Mick replied. 'John! You in range yet?'

'If you'd bother to have asked, we have been for ages, but I didn't know what my target was since you were busy doing your fancy acrobatics!'

'Ok, keep your navy cap on! Target the wheels. Try to get it to sink into the water.'

'Sure, we'll try, but we have incoming missiles; a lot of them.'

Mick looked up again. Hundreds and hundreds of small missiles were hurtling towards them.

'Eeks!' Mick cried. He dived out of the way of the one that was almost directly on his head.

He looked round. He had forgotten to warn his comrades, but his 'eek' had been heard over the speaker, and they had realized the danger before the rain of missiles had hit them.

After about a minute, there was a slight relapse in the assault. In that time, his second in command, Charlie, called on Mick and said,

'Do you know you said "eeks"?'

'Did I really say "eeks"? That is just such a bad... just a really bad... "uh-oh" word.'

'Uh-oh word? Mick, you really have gone nuts.'

'Well I was never sane before, if you noticed.'

'Don't you worry. We all did.'

'Alright clever clogs just get on with the job.'

'Ok boss, I'm going.' He moved away slightly, mocking him. Unfortunately, he did not see the small missile hurtling out of the sky directly towards him.

Mick did, however.

'Watch out Charlie! Full throttle forward!' Charlie did as Mick said, but he was just too late, the missile clipped the back end of his plane. The missile didn't explode, but Charlie had lost his engine none the less.

'Mick, my velocity is going to take me right into the top of the target. My flaps have gone, so I won't survive. It was nice knowing you!'

'Oh no you don't!' Mick said. 'Squadron, stay here and watch our backs. Come down if you need, but **only** if you need to. Got that?'

'Yes, sir.'

With nothing else to take care of, Mick dived after Charlie. Charlie had got a little way ahead already, but Mick caught up with him quickly.

'Charlie, lower your landing wheels!'

'Sure thing, but how will that help?'

'Just do it!'

Charlie answered by letting three wheels protrude from the underside of his plane.

They were getting closer and closer to the target. Mick got in line with Charlie so he was flying straight down right next under him. He lined it up so his nose was pushing Charlie's front wheel. He pushed up and up very gently so that Charlie's plane was no longer heading straight down, but was slightly tilted upwards.

They got even closer to the target. Soon they were so close that collision was imminent.

But that was not so with Mick Denning. He pushed hard on his joystick and propelled himself up so that he was level again. Charlie had also been pushed into that position and was now sitting on top of Mick's plane.

The ele-metal that the plane was made of was very strong, so it could take the weight of another fighter and a half!

Mick flew on over the target and over the other side, right above a line of electricity. He flew on.

With guns starting to fire upon him, Mick decided it was time to turn round. He had to go slowly or risk losing Charlie. But that would make them sitting ducks for the enemy batteries. He explained this problem to Charlie. Luckily he had a plan.

'Since my shields are still working, we can merge them. That will make them much stronger. And if we fly further away, not all the batteries will be able to hit us!'

It was an ingenious plan, and Mick went to it straight away. Charlie got his shields to merge with Mick's and, when out of range of some of the batteries, they turned round, very slowly. After about five minutes they had turned round a whole 180 degrees.

But not without injury. A few shots had got through the shields, all aimed at Mick. Now the plane was slightly weakened, and it was starting to feel the strain.

But Mick was still surprised at how little shots had actually hit them, shields and all. Once he had turned all the way round he had found out why.

The rest of the squadron had come down and distracted the fire of the enemy. They had been clever as they had come down only over the batteries that were able to fire at them. None of them had been shot. Mick got on the comm. and said,

'Hey, guys, thanks for that. But you can pull off now. It will be safer.'

'Aww, but we're having so much fun!' Jimmy said, but they pulled up anyway.

Mick now increased speed, but his plane started to creak. He wasn't going to make it to land, but they might make...

'Charlie, I'm going to land on the target.'

'WHAT?! Are you crazy?'

Mick gave a sigh. 'I've already discussed this with you; yes, I am. But there is no time to argue. My jet is not going to hold the strain much longer. The only place I can reach is the target.'

'What about the water?' Charlie asked.

'Never liked water. You can sink in it.' Mick replied.

So Mick headed towards the target. He was now flying directly beside the streaming electricity. He wondered how much of the U.K. and France had lost its electricity.

But Mick was now just below the flat top. He headed up slightly. Then, just before he reached it, he dipped back down and then, with an increase of speed, suddenly up right in front of a battery.

He halted in mid-air. Charlie went flying off just over and onto the flat top of the target. Mick fired a concussion missile into the battery, flew vertically up and landed next to Charlie, cleanly and neatly.

'Phew, that was hot going!' Charlie exclaimed as he got out of his cockpit.

'Yeah, it sure was.' Mick agreed. 'And it's not over yet,' he added, as he saw a trap door open a little way off.

Two men came out. One of them was large and muscly. The other was a boy dressed in the black robes of a karate black belt.

Tomodan and The Evil San had come to greet them.

'Why, hello there!' The Evil San said. 'Welcome, to my base. Again. I am sorry that you had to come at such an inappropriate time, so I guess I have to ask you to leave. If you don't, I will ask my friend here to force you.'

'What do you mean, force us?' Charlie asked. Since he had never seen the San before he did not know who the person he was talking to was.

'Force you...off the edge.'

'That is not...' but then realization hit him.

'Wait a minute, are you the Evil San?'

'Well, I guess I am known by that name, yes.' The Evil San seemed bored. 'Look, are you going to leave or not?'

'I'm not; Charlie is.' Mick replied.

Charlie looked shocked. 'Why aren't you?' He asked.

'I have a little feud to deal with.'

'No mate, you really should leave.'

'I don't have plane. And anyway, I am going to settle this once and for all.'

'Well, good luck mate. I'll try and give you a hand.'

'No you can't, because you are leaving in my plane and heading back to base and telling the commander-in-chief what has happened.'

'That does not mean I can't lend a hand.' Charlie whispered. He jumped into the fighter and put the cockpit cover down. He raised a hand in farewell. Mick did the same. Charlie took off.

Mick turned round to fight what he presumed would be his final battle. As he did, he thought of Katrina. He wondered if she would miss him. He just wanted to talk to her one more time, but he knew that wasn't possible. But hey, that was the fortunes of war.

But he did not mind, since he knew he would go to a better place.

He turned round.

'Woah!' Suddenly, Tomodan was there, not 3 feet away. Mick took a step back to recover from the shock.

But Tomodan was already moving forwards to attack him. Mick ran towards the broken fighter still on the rock. Tomodan chased him. He was very fast and had just about caught Mick when Mick jumped up. He hit the side of the plane with his foot, absorbed the impact, and then pushed off with all the force he had. Turning himself at the same time, he smashed his foot right under Tomodan's chin. He went flying. Since the novenicity in the plane had still been on, some of it had flowed through him and into Tomodan as he was struck.

Tomodan flew ten feet in the air and hit the ground hard. He wasn't too far from the edge. He started to get up, but suddenly an explosion hit the area near to where Tomodan had been lying. The explosion threw Tomodan up in the air. He landed on the rock and rolled.

'NO!' The Evil San yelled. But Tomodan did not hear. He didn't see the edge of the rock and fell off the edge.

There was no scream, just a silence.

Mick looked up. There, just flying away from the battle scene was his fighter.

Now all that was left was him and the Evil San.

'Well well, the final showdown is between me and you, Unknown Kid. I always thought it might. But it does not matter, for you will lose. It is a shame. Are you sure you don't want to reinstate our friendship?'

'Oh, I'm sure. I have friends, that are loyal to the last, and with them, I will fight on and on and nothing will stop me with the thought that you are still out in the open!' Mick felt strong.

'Pity.' The San said simply, and then he readied himself. So did Mick. For a moment they stood still, in a battle of wills.

Then they flew at each other. Mick fought hard, but from the moment they came into contact, Mick knew he was outclassed by far. He was very good at martial arts, but the San was perfect. He knew every form and could execute it at a professional level, just as he said. Mick got thrown off his feet time and time again, but never did he give up, he fought on and on.

Eventually, Mick got a kick to the groin. He bent over double, and got a punch in the chest, sending him up in the air, and then a kick to the stomach sending him far, far across the flat topped rock. This time Mick did not get up, but lay there in pain. He was right by the edge, his head over the edge. As he looked down, he saw the battle raging, and wondered for a moment,

'*Why?*'

He was ready to give up and accept his fate, but then he saw something hanging from his neck. It was his shark tooth necklace. Suddenly, he found himself smiling.

'*Maybe,*' he thought, '*this isn't quite the end after all.*'

He got up from the floor, turned to face the San, and knelt down. He put the beads of the necklace in his mouth so that the tooth was just sticking out from his mouth. Then he laced his hands together and closed his eyes.

'What are you doing?' The San asked.

'Brayin,' Mick mumbled.

'What?'

He took the shark tooth out of his mouth.

'Praying.' He put it back in, squeezing it with his lips a little as he did so.

'*One,*' Mick thought.

'Oh,' the San said, a little taken aback. 'And why, may I ask?'

Mick, frustrated, took the shark tooth out of his mouth again.

'Because I am accepting my fate.'

Now the Evil San's confusion went, and a realization came with a wicked grin.

'So you have realized your fate is death, then. Well, since I am a man of honour, I will let you finish your prayer, and then I will kill you.'

Mick put the shark tooth back in his mouth again.

'*Two,*' he said to himself.

'*Lord, please let this work,*' Mick prayed.

His eyes popped open with a fire kindled in them. The Evil San was waiting.

'I am ready for you.' Mick said. It was hard though, because he still had the tooth in his mouth.

'So now I can finish this.' The Evil San said.

'No, let me.' Mick said. He squeezed the tooth a third time.

'Wha..?' The Evil San just about got out before he had a thin tooth sticking out of his neck. He looked puzzled, and then he fell to the floor.

Mick had conquered the Evil San.

But suddenly, the whole rock lurched. Mick was thrown off the edge, but he just grabbed on in time. He hung on to the edge for dear life.

He looked down. The tyres had been burst, and the machinery had fallen into the sea.

It was an impressive sight. All of the novenicity was either blowing up or was short circuiting.

'*All electrical things short out in water. No different with novenicity.*' Mick thought.

The place lurched again as all the electricity that had been stolen broke out of the rock. It burst out of the centre of the rock and went in all directions. Now the top section was being held up by a few pillars. The whole place was doomed, and Mick was about to fall.

But, out of nowhere a face appeared.

'Need a hand?' It said. He held one out.

Mick grabbed the hand without even thinking. Eventually, he found himself back on his own two feet.

Now that he wasn't quite so busy wondering whether he was going to die or not, he was able to get a better look at the man who had rescued him. He recognized the face.

'Thanks.' Was all he could say.

'You're welcome.' The man said. 'I am Dr. Feanam by the way.'

'Right, well, Dr. Feanam, I think we had better get off this rock, as it seems like it is going to collapse.'

'Um, and how are we going to do that?' He asked sarcastically.

'By catching a lift!' Mick replied, as he pointed up in the sky.

There, a helicopter was coming in to land. As it landed, a side door opened and someone beckoned at them to get in. They did not need to be told twice. Two men got out and ran to the body of the Evil San, picked it up, and dumped in the back of the chopper.

They jumped in, and the door was slammed shut. The pilot took off. The person who was in the back with them took off their helmet and shook their red hair out of their eyes.

'Katrina!' Mick yelled (for you had to yell to be heard), and he gave her a big hug.

The Mop-up

'Well, Mick, it seems like you are in a bit of trouble.'

It was the next day, and Mick, John, and Katrina had gone to see the boss. It was very rare for this to happen, but they had been given this privilege since it was their first big mission, and it had been a very big mission.

'Since you were in charge, all the blame has been laid upon you.'

'What blame?' Mick was confused and, he admitted, a little frightened. He had just saved the world from being sent into the Dark Ages, and all he got was a telling off!

'What did I do wrong?'

'You did nothing wrong, exactly. It is just that the government needs to blame someone, and the Evil San, in their opinion, is just a boy.' The boss explained.

'But so am I!'

'I know. But they have seen the amazing feats you have achieved. They have not seen the Evil Sans'. The boss gave a little grin. 'At least, not yet anyway.'

Mick just deflated. He knew he was going to be blamed for a lot. He just hoped that the majority of the public would be on his side.

'But what about the big machine? They can't say that wasn't the Evil San?' Mick complained.

'They say it was Tomodan and Dr. Feanam,' the boss replied. 'I have been meaning to ask you - what happened to Tomodan?

'He dropped off.' Mick said.

The boss looked a little confused but left it alone.

'What have I got against me, then,' Mick said dejectedly.

'Here it says that you have been charged with the damage that was caused by the Evil San coming from the depths and the damage to the ships in the ocean when it landed.'

'What does that mean I need to do? Do I need to pay for this?'

No. It just means we have to pay for it and to give you a warning,' he said. 'I am warning you not to do such things again. There, you have been warned.'

Mick was surprised. 'Is that it?' He asked.

'Well, some of the people who have been hurt by this might hold a grudge, so I would consider moving schools. The damage caused near the garage was rather severe, so it might be dangerous, even though they do not know who you are.'

'Yes, boss.'

'And now,' the boss continued, as he walked round the table, 'to you two.'

'Yes boss?' They said simultaneously.

'I would like to thank you for your help with this mission. I would also like to tell you, Katrina, that the army would be glad to give a place in the higher ranks. They were very impressed with your tactical planning.'

'Thanks a lot!' Katrina said. 'That would be really cool. But how did they know it was me?'

'A certain commanding officer happened to let you slip to his boss.' The boss said cheekily.

He turned to the window.

'You have all done very well, and I hope to find you some other 'men' for you soon.' Katrina giggled. The boss gave her a frown. 'You can go.'

They all got up to leave. John and Katrina left, but as Mick reached the door, the boss called to him.

'Mick, wait a moment please.'

Mick stopped.

'Err, well, this has been a pretty major event, and the press has been asking questions. They say they saw two boys fighting on the top of the rock, and they want answers. Is it ok if we tell them a secure and brief account of what happened?'

'Sure boss.' He turned to leave.

'Wait!'

'Yes?'

'We will need to give you an alias; a codename if you wish. Do you have any ideas?'

Mick thought for a moment. Then,

'The Unknown Kid,' he said.

'That will do.' Mick turned to leave again.

'And Mick?!'

'Yes?' Mick said impatiently.

'Congratulations.' He said it softly, as though he meant it personally. Mick had never heard that before. He gave a little smile.

'Thanks chief.' He walked out of the room.

Katrina and John had waited at the entrance for him. Together, they walked towards the station. As they did, Mick thought about the past few days.

How could Gareth have gone so wrong? Mick really did not know how so much could have been addled by a simple electric shock.

'*But then, life is never simple*.' Mick thought.

'Are you alright Mick?' Katrina asked.

Mick looked round. They had made their way to the Tube entrance, and somehow John had wondered off.

'Mick?' She asked again.

'Yeah, I'm fine.' Mick said. 'Hey, do you want to go for a coffee?'

'Oh, are you asking me out on a date, now?'

'Maybe, I am, but I wouldn't tell you if I was, would I? You should know.' He gave her a cheeky grin.

'Ok, sure. I'll have a tea, though.' Katrina replied, also with a grin.

So off they went (eventually hand in hand) to grab a drink.

In the store next to the coffee shop, however, Mick saw a TV which showed a home video of the action that had taken place the other day. Mick assumed this is how people saw what had happened.

He watched it for a bit. He saw himself fighting the Evil San. And then suddenly it skipped. The rock lurched as another tyre burst, and the camera zoomed into a boy hanging from the top. A spot light hit him, and then the film faded out. A message popped up which read,

THANKYOU UNKNOWN KID,
WHEREVER YOU ARE!

Mick smiled and thought,

'I am already famous! And it seems we both have the same taste in name choosing!' He moved on.

As they were about to walk into the corner shop, Mick heard a scream from a side street just across the road.

'Go on. Go be my hero.' Katrina whispered in his ear.

So Mick Denning, number three spy for the S.P.F.T., champion over the Evil San, and a.k.a. the Unknown Kid, walked off, to live the life he had been destined for.